GERDA STEVENSON is an award-winning writer, actor, theatre director and singer-songwriter. She has worked on stage, television, radio, film and in opera, throughout the UK and abroad, and is a recipient of Scottish Arts Council and Creative Scotland writers' bursaries. Her stage play, *Federer Versus Murray*, directed by the author, toured to New York in 2012, and was published there by Salmagundi. In 2014 she was nominated as Scots Singer of the Year for the MG Alba Scots Trad Music Awards, following the launch of an album of her own songs *Night Touches Day*. She has written extensively for radio, including original plays and dramatisations of Scottish novels. Her poetry collections, *If This Were Real* (Smokestack Books, 2013), and *Quines: Poems in Tribute to Women of Scotland* (Luath Press, 1st edition 2018, 2nd edition 2020) have been published in Rome by Edizioni Ensemble in Italian translations by Laura Maniero, 2017 and 2021, respectively. She wrote the biographical introduction and a series of poems for the book *Inside & Out: The Art of Christian Small*, (Scotland Street Press, 2019). She collaborated with Scottish landscape photographer Allan Wright on their book *Edinburgh*, for which she wrote the introduction and a sequence of twenty-two poems (Allan Wright Photographic, 2019). In 2021, she directed a film of George Mackay Brown's play *The Storm Watchers*, for the St Magnus International Festival. A seasoned performer, she won a BAFTA Best Film Actress award for her role in Margaret Tait's feature film *Blue Black Permanent*, and is the founder of Stellar Quines, Scotland's leading women's theatre company.

By the same same author:

Poetry:
*If This Were Real* (Smokestack Books, 2013)
Se Questo Fosse Vero / *If This Were Real* (Edizioni Ensemble, Rome, 2017)
*Quines: Poems in Tribute to Women of Scotland* (Luath Press, 1st edition 2018, 2nd edition 2020)
*Quines: Tributo poetico a donne della Scozia* (Edizioni Ensemble, 2021)
*Inside & Out: The Art of Christian Small*, with an introduction and poems by Gerda Stevenson (Lyne Press, 2018; Scotland Street Press, 2019)
Edinburgh (Allan Wright Photographic, 2019)

Plays for stage:
*Pentlands at War*, a community play, co-written with the Pentlands Writers' Group (Scottish Borders Council Library Services, 2006)
*Federer Versus Murray* (Salmagundi, USA, 2012)

For children:
*The Candlemaker and Other Stories*, illustrated by the author (Kahn & Averill, 1987)

# Letting Go

## A timeline of tales

*For Pam*

GERDA STEVENSON

*best wishes —*

*Gerda Stevenson*

**Luath** Press Limited

EDINBURGH

www.luath.co.uk

First published 2021

ISBN: 978-1-910022-91-7

The author's right to be identified as author of this book
under the Copyright, Designs and Patents Act 1988 has been asserted.

The paper used in this book is recyclable. It is made
from low chlorine pulps produced in a low energy,
low emissions manner from renewable forests.

Printed and bound by
Robertson Printers, Forfar

Typeset in 10.5 point Sabon by
Main Point Books, Edinburgh

# Contents

Graves                                    9

Bella Day                                 23

Letting Go                                41

Colour                                    49

The Apple Tree                            67

Chromosomes and Chocolate                 89

A Day Off                                 99

Merryland Street                          113

The Fiver                                 123

The Grail                                 131

A Botanical Curiosity for Eve             141

Skeleton Wumman                           155

Acknowledgements                          169

Scots Glossary                            171

In memory of Marilyn Imrie,
inspirational catalyst, collaborator,
and encourager.

# Graves

SARAH WAS PERCHED on top of a ladder, leaning against the gallery, paintbrush in hand. The vestry door opened below, and an autumn gust swept into the quiet kirk, billowing her long skirts. A man entered in a cloud of leaves.

'Hello?' she called down to him, flustered, trying to smooth the air from her petticoats without getting paint everywhere.

He looked up at her. 'Thought ye were an angel, there, missus!'

She observed him from her perch. He was broad shouldered, but slim, with a tousie mass of black hair. His face, as their eyes met, had an open look about it, she thought, like a moorland road. 'Can I help?' she asked.

'I'm in hopes ye can,' he said, scanning the pews.

She wrapped the paintbrush in a cloth, laid it on the gallery ledge, and with her back to him, descended the ladder, one hand holding up her skirts to avoid tripping. She was sure his eyes were examining every inch of her exposed ankles and shins.

'Never seen a leddy up a ladder afore,' he smiled, and offered his hand, which she didn't take, as she stepped onto the floor from the last rung. 'No yin o the gentry at ony rate.' He surveyed the gallery, where she'd been highlighting the biblical texts in gold leaf. 'Bonnie wood-work. Some skill, yon carvin.'

'Thank you,' she said, glad of the compliment.

'Whit – ye done it yersel? Aa thae vines? Aa thae wee falderals o thistles and wheat and…?' His words tailed off in amazement.

'Not *all* by myself – my sister too.'

He took hold of her hands. She pulled away, but he held on with firmness, and turned them over in his, as if appraising a set of priceless new tools. She was well into her twenties, but no man had ever touched her, let alone held her like this. His skin was dark as peat against hers, and sent a shiver through her stomach.

'Fine fingers ye have, missus – strang and canny, yet gentle wi it. And yer palms – like tough, white silk.'

'Our father's a surgeon,' she replied, extracting herself at last from his grip.

'So I've heard. And tae the Queen hersel.'

'Yes. People say we get it from him, the precision of the scalpel.'

'Weel, wood is a kind o flesh, that's true. I work wi willow masel. Baskets.'

'Ah,' she said. 'You're a hawker?'

'That's no why I'm here.'

'Are you looking for someone, then?'

'I am.' He seemed to be hinting she should know. His breath quickened.

'Well?' she prompted.

He pinned her with his eyes. 'For the man that killed ma mither.'

They stood in silence for a moment as she tried to take this in.

'But… but why here?'

'Weel, nae maiter,' he sighed, as if suddenly dismissing the subject. 'Are ye needin ony baskets? I've a few in ma cairt.'

'Oh, so you *are* a hawker!'

'I hae tae earn a livin,' he said simply.

Politeness prevailed as she recovered her composure: 'I'd

like to see your baskets, yes,' and she moved towards the door.

'Naw, naw!' he called over his shoulder, sweeping past her. 'I'll bring them in. Nae pynt staunin aboot in the cauld. The deil's fair blawin up a bleester oot there!'

Sarah doubted he was looking for his mother's killer – more likely a sales strategy to elicit sympathy. He returned with four baskets – two on each arm.

'These are well made,' she said, fingering the firm weave. 'I like this one – perfect for gathering mushrooms. My old basket's a bit battered with use.'

'The right season fur it,' he nodded.

'It is. The birch woods over the burn are full of chantarelles and ceps right now.'

'Horn o plenty's the best – yon black curly yin. Grows unner beech trees.'

'Trumpet of Death, the French call it.'

'Daith?' he repeated, a glimmer of challenge in his smile.

'Yes. Trompette de la Mort,' she found herself elaborating, though somehow wished she hadn't.

'Should be *life*,' he replied. 'They're full o goodness – a hale meal in a single bite.'

She'd only a few coppers in her skirt pocket to pay for the basket, but he accepted what she had, and agreed to bring another of the same design a day or two later for her sister. He was camped in the hills, he said, doing seasonal work as a navvy on the new reservoir, which would power the paper mills in the nearby town. 'There's three hunner o us workin up there. Irish, maistly, an a hantle o us traivellers.'

Sarah had heard something of this, and with dismay. The reservoir was once a small loch, her childhood playground on unforgettable summer days. Father used to fish there, and sometimes, as a treat, when Mother was well enough, he hired a carter to take the family with him. The housekeeper prepared a hamper, and Mother spread the feast on a linen cloth, white as a cloud, its lace edges fluttering like moths in the grass. The girls stripped to their camisoles and bloomers, and swam in the clear water under a blue sky. 'I know that place,' she told the traveller. 'I used to swim out to a small island there.'

'The yin wi the seven graves?'

'Yes – like stone beds,' she said, intrigued and delighted that he seemed so familiar with a part of the world she loved. The graves had appeared one year after a huge storm washed the topsoil away.

'They'll be unner watter soon, when the dam's finished.'

'My sister and I used to lie in them, and pretend we were dead – a sin, I'm sure!'

'Could be,' he agreed. 'Daith's no juist a game.'

She blushed then, at her *faux pas* in returning to the subject, but blundered on, flustered. 'Ancient burial kists, my father told us.'

'Oh, aye,' he said with a dark look. 'Yer faither wud ken aa aboot graves.'

Four days passed, and still he hadn't come with the promised second basket. Sarah tried, but couldn't put this man and their meeting from her mind. He'd unsettled her. She found it hard to concentrate.

Time was her own these days, since her sister Margaret had married, and the church project hers to complete. Father was away in London most of the year. Mother spent much of her time in bed – always had done, though the sisters were never quite sure why. 'The curse,' Mrs Pennel, the housekeeper would say mysteriously, with no further explanation, like that time, when they were young girls, and wandered into the laundry.

Mrs P was rubbing strips of linen in a basin of reddish-pink water that looked like blood. 'Awa wi ye!' she called, shooing them out of the door. 'Ye're ower young fur kennin the curse!'

Every month, the strips would hang like fillets of pale skin pegged on a line in the laundry – never outside with the rest of the washing. Sarah thought she was going to die when, as a girl of thirteen, she woke up one morning to find her bed sheet blotted with scarlet.

'The curse,' said Mrs P. 'Comes tae us aa, lassie. Noo, oot ye get!' and she pulled the stained sheet from under her. 'Awa and gie yersel a wash, and I'll fetch the strips fur ye.'

When she handed them to her, Sarah wondered if they were the same ones they'd seen her scrubbing that day in the laundry. They did look faintly pink. She shuddered at the thought of her mother's diluted blood, dried particles locked into those linen threads, lurking there and mingling with her own. You could never wash blood away, no matter how hard you tried, especially from these tattered emblems of shame.

'I suppose a dish of chanterelles might tempt my appetite,' Mother sighed wanly, propped up against a huge pile of pillows banked like clouds. Sarah had brought the new basket up to the bedroom to show her.

But she didn't want to miss the traveller calling by. So, despite her fractured concentration, and her guilt at not responding to her mother's wistful hint, Sarah decided against foraging for the time being, and got on with her work. She climbed the ladder to measure up the West window in preparation for designing the final ivy border. And she still had the gilding of the texts around the gallery to complete. There were eleven in all, each set in an oak panel, carved with images from nature – abundant grapes hanging from tendrils for *I am the vine – ye are the branches*, and sheaves of wheat for *Give us this day our daily bread*. The last was her favourite – mournful willows bending around the words *Weep with them that weep*. They expressed well the tender exhortation of the text, she felt, and reminded her of the song Mrs P always sang when she was ironing:

> *Why weep ye by the tide, lady,*
> *Why weep ye by the tide,*
> *I'll wad ye tae ma youngest son,*
> *And ye shall be his bride.*
> *And ye shall be his bride, lady,*
> *Sae comely tae be seen.*

The last line of the melody had a weeping downward flow, like her carved willows:

> *But aye she loot the tears doonfaa*
> *For Jock o Hazeldean.*

A whole week passed, then two. The weather was fine, and Sarah decided to head for the woods. But inviting as they were, birch leaves kindling to an autumn blaze, she passed them by, her basket empty, and made for the hills, up to the reservoir. After a couple of miles, an unfamiliar sound filtered through the still air – almost industrial, she thought, as she drew nearer – a cacophony of ringing metal, the rumble of wheels, and voices calling – singing, even. As she rounded the last bend in the track, she saw a crowd of men digging. Horses were pulling carts loaded with huge stones. The march of progress, she thought ruefully, watching her childhood idyll being ripped apart and restructured by an army. The reality was much more shocking than she'd imagined. A group of women and children sang as they stamped the ground rhythmically in a muddy basin gouged out of the loch-side.

'That's the overflow,' said a voice at her shoulder. She swung round, and there he was – her traveller, spade in hand. 'I spied ye comin up the hill, yer hat bobbin aa the way. I thocht it micht be you.'

She hadn't seen him approach, so intent she'd been on the scene. 'What are those women and children doing?'

'Trampling the grun – puddle clay, we cry it – watterproof when it's spreid oot flat tae mak a clean surface. They're aa fitted wi shoon fur the job, by the consortium, ken – the mill owners. First and last thae fowk'll ever see o guid leather on their feet.'

Tents were pitched close to the loch, smoke coiling from workers' camp fires.

'Do you have family here?' she asked, with the sudden realisation that he might be married.

'I'm on ma ain,' was his oblique response. 'I havenae made it doon tae see ye this past week – the foreman's giein a real push wi the wark while the weather's braw. But I've got yer basket.'

'I mustn't hold you back.'

'Naw, naw, I can tak a wee break, shairly,' and he led her to his tent, a hazel bender, with blankets neatly wrapped round the frame. A fire burned outside under a tripod of carefully cut sticks, a steaming pot hanging from them on a willow loop. He opened the door flap, and she glanced inside. His make-shift home was arranged with simple care – a narrow bed of straw, a wooden box next to it, and various tools. A pile of baskets lay in one corner.

'Come in,' he said, beckoning her. 'Choose the yin ye fancy.'

She hesitated. This tent was his bedroom. A whistle went up from a lad walking past with a spade on his shoulder. 'Entertainin the gentry, are we now, Duncan?' he teased, with an Irish lilt, and gave her a wink.

She blushed scarlet, and turned away. 'I must be getting back,' she told the traveller. 'I don't need another basket, really.'

He followed her along the track, until a shout from the foreman called him to his work. 'Guid tae see ye, miss... sorry – I dinnae ken yer name.' He took her hand. 'As ye juist heard tell, I'm Duncan.'

'Sarah.' Her cheeks reddened again – why on earth had she been so familiar as to give him her Christian name!

'Well, Sarah. I hope it winnae be lang till next we meet.'

That dark inquisition behind his eyes troubled and thrilled her. She blushed even deeper, and scurried off down the hill, stopping by the woods to fill her basket with chanterelles. Their golden heads nestling among tree roots in the dappled leafy light calmed her hectic mind. She knelt down and pushed her fingers into the damp moss to feel for each stem's base, gently lifting the fluted flesh from its bed. Her senses tingled with pleasure.

Another week went by. All she could think of was Duncan. Until now, she'd assumed her life was set in stone: the unmarried eldest daughter, her sickly mother's companion, and local upholder of her absent father's reputation. Her sister Margaret had always been the one to draw attention – lively, confident and beautiful with her long auburn plaits and wide set, sky blue eyes. Everything about her was vibrant. Sarah, her father once said, cuttingly, was 'a mousy brown creature of the shadows'; though Mother offered the dubious consolation that her tall stature and mysterious grey eyes were saving graces.

The congregation frowned on the sisters' wood carving, deemed an unsuitable occupation for women. But Sarah loved it – the pungent smell of wood shavings in the shed where she worked next to the house, set out with all the tools she needed. Her own domain. It filled her with satisfaction, though dangerously close to pride – the alchemy of graven images. She knew this was why it wasn't talked of at home. But the minister, now Margaret's husband, had approved the project. He'd seen and praised the carving practised by the sisters since their teens, when he was a frequent visitor. Locally he was considered to be suspiciously liberal, tolerated only because of his standing. Sarah liked him, and the church carving went ahead largely due to his endorsement. After several years it was now nearing completion, though over the last eighteen months the work had been entirely Sarah's. Since her marriage, Margaret had lost all interest in their joint endeavour. An uncomfortable distance had crept into the sisters' relationship, and Sarah struggled sometimes with resentment.

The low chime of the grandfather clock in the hall was the loneliest sound she could think of, especially when she sat on her own every evening, served by Mrs P at the huge mahogany dining table. She watched her fingers articulating the ranks of heavy silver cutlery, and remembered how Duncan had held her hands in his, and admired them, when they first met. She found herself examining the white skin of her slender wrists peeping through her lace cuffs. There was no mirror in the house – vanity couldn't be countenanced – but right now she wished there was – a full length one. Thinking of Duncan made her want to see herself without clothes on. A new moistness seeped between her thighs – pleasureable – different from the shameful monthly bleed.

One night, when she was getting ready for bed, she took the candle to the darkened window, and looked at her naked body reflected in the glass. The curve of her breasts, the sweep of waistline down to hips and thighs pleased her – a sin, she knew it, but was it so *very* different from the way the shapes she'd carved in the church gave her pleasure? She wondered if her brother-in-law, the minister, had ever seen her sister like this. She was certain her father had never looked at her mother unclothed. She couldn't imagine it possible, although he must have seen many naked bodies in the anatomy class at medical school. Strange, it occurred to her, that given her father's profession, the human body and its functions were never discussed at home.

Duncan wanted something from her, she could see that in his eyes, although she couldn't fathom what it might be. Was it really to do with his mother's death, or could it be herself he wanted – this naked vision, gleaming in the dark glass?

The last carved ivy vine now fringed the lower half of the West window. Sarah was pleased with the flowing lines – the tendrils appeared to grow with a lovely grace towards the apex of the arch. Her work was finished, and she'd been at a loose end for days. At night she was restless – couldn't sleep.

A harvest moon hung like a blood orange above the hills. She decided to take a walk before bed, down the brae to the kirk graveyard. From above the wall, before she entered, she could already see the obelisk that soared at the centre, the monument proclaiming her ancestor's pre-eminence – part of an imposing stone enclosure with its own elaborate iron gate. She read the names – lawyers, medics, their wives and daughters. She'd be buried there herself one day, she supposed.

'Shairly ye're no thinkin o leavin us?'

She spun round to find Duncan at her shoulder again, reading her thoughts, it seemed.

'Will we sit doon on yon grave?' he asked, pointing to one that lay outside her family's enclosure, flat like a bed on stone supports. The image of a couple was carved on its surface – a young man and woman holding hands in their last, eternal sleep. No names marked their short lives, and Sarah had always wondered who they were. Some said brother and sister, but she was certain they were lovers. Duncan took her hand: 'Come on, I'm shair they'll no mind!'

She sat next to him on the cold grave in the moonlight.

'What is it you want from me?' she asked, her heart beating so loud she was sure he must hear it.

'Och,' he sighed, as if expelling a dead weight from his core, 'I thocht I kent, but I'm no sae shair noo. I'm that weary o it aa.'

'Is it about your mother?'

'Aye. It is.'

'I'm sorry.'

'Well, it *wis*, but noo... did ye ken yer faither warked wi thon anatomist, Dr Knox in Edinburgh toon? The yin that bocht the bodies frae the burkers – the grave snatchers?'

She'd heard rumours, she told him, that was all. She'd once asked her mother about it. But the question was ignored, the frosty response simply that her father was a baronet.

'And whan they ran oot o graves tae herry, the burkers, as we cry them, they took tae murderin fowk – traivellers, they went fur, *ma* fowk, and sauld them tae the medics. Your faither wis in chairge o gettin the bodies frae the burkers, and peyin fur them.'

'My father – payed for...?'

'Aye. That's richt.'

'And your mother – she was...?'

Her father knew the Commandments. He'd seen the panel she and Margaret had carved in the gallery – the words *Thou Shalt Not Kill* featured there. He'd even praised the finesse of their representation. He was trained to preserve life – not collude in its obliteration. Oh, she was familiar with the arguments – how could surgeons learn the science without the raw material to practice on? Perhaps that's how he'd seen this man's mother. Raw flesh. The biblical texts she'd carved splintered into meaningless fragments in her mind.

'I've hud a kind o mission since I wis a bairn, when I lost ma mither tae the burkers. I've askit the hale country ower whaur Maister Knox and yer faither micht be fund. But they're aye in London toon, I'm tellt; and I hae mair chance o findin gowd in a midden.'

'I'm sorry – I really am,' she said, hating herself for emphasising what she felt was such an inadequate response.

He looked her straight in the eye. 'I heard yer faither's faimily bide hereaboots, so I cam tae hae it oot wi you insteid.'

She felt implicated somehow, by association, and wondered whether her sister knew about this horror. They sat in silence till it occurred to her that the timing of his appearance tonight was strange. 'Why have you come so late?'

'I'm leavin the wark at the reservoir.'

'What – leaving tonight?'

'Aye. It's a slave business they're runnin up there. I'm ma ain maister. I'm movin on.'

She was sure he was looking at her with something more like gladness than accusation. 'Why did you not have it out with me sooner, that day in the kirk, when you first came here?'

'Och, lass,' he said. 'Ye took the wund oot ma sails.'

'How? I don't understand.' She'd been the one with the wind in her sails that day, she remembered, the way it went blowing up her petticoats when he opened the kirk door!

'Wi yer bonnie carvin, that's how, an yer bonnie face.'

She wanted to say she'd go with him, leave this place and join him on the open road. She felt certain he'd say 'Yes', that this was what he wanted of her now. The words of Mrs Pennel's song came to her, the final verse:

*They socht her baith by bower and haa,*
*The lady wasnae seen,*
*She's ower the border and awa*
*Wi Jock o Hazeldean.*

Her mother would be calling, as she always did, last thing at night, asking her to rearrange the pillows, to read a passage from the bible.

He took her hands in his, just as he'd done on the day they first met, turning them over, her palms white in the moonlight. It was as if he was reacquainting himself with every detail of something precious he'd lost and found, and was about to lose again. Then he let them go and stood up. 'Weel, that's me, lass. I'll be on ma way.'

She watched him leave the graveyard, heard him call 'gee up' to his horse, heard the hooves and cart wheels fading on the night air.

'Wait!' she called after him, and she ran and ran, all the way down the road till she caught up with him. 'Please – wait!'

'Whoa!' he called, and the horse stopped.

'I want to come with you,' she heard herself say, breathless with running, clutching the shaft of the cart.

'Are ye shair, lass?' was all he asked.

'Yes,' she said.

He held out his hand, and pulled her up next to him.

'I'm sure. I've finished with everything here.'

# Bella Day

SEE ROSEHIPS? I used tae go doon the Deanfoot Road every dinnertime tae pick them, for the vitamin C, tae send them awa for the syrup. Daein ma bit for the war. Funny, tae think o thae fat red rubies, full o lifeblood, ripenin in the sun, while bombs were drappin, and blood runnin oot oor lads in spates.

I'd get a roll frae Haldane's, or sometimes frae Russell the Bakers. It's aye quiet at dinnertime, the village goes dead sleepy. Just the chug, chug, o the trains goin up and doon the moor tae the munitions store at Macbiehill. And the birds. I like the soond o the geese best. Maks me think o far awa places. I'd like tae go tae a far awa place. Used tae wish I wis on a silver beach in the sun, when I wis workin in MacFarlane's Drapers. It's that dark in there. Dark wood o the coonter and the shop cupboards. And Miss MacPhail. She wis aye that nippy wi me:

'Now don't you *dare* be back late, Mary! I want the floor swept and washed this afternoon. And the glass doors dusted down.'

'Right-oh, Miss MacPhail.'

It wis nice tae get oot. The roll could hae done wi a bit butter, though. And a banana would hae been just dandy – lang wedges sliced in the middle – but we hadnae seen a banana for years, no since the rations came in. There wis a guid crop o rosehips, mind. They'd reached their best that day, ripened full and fat, and I wis fillin up ma broon paper poke.

'Buon giorno, signorina!'

I nearly jumped oot ma skin! A dark-haired man wis sittin by the roadside, eatin a cooked tattie. I hadnae seen him – he wis leanin back in the sun, by a rose bush, near the gate tae Robinsland Farm.

'Che bella giornata!'

'Eh – whit?' I didnae ken whit he wis on aboot. Made nae sense. He waved his airms at the blue sky, and smiled at me.

'Bella.'

Bella. I'd heard it afore – a lassie's name.

'Bella. Like you!'

'Oh... aye.' The penny drapped. I went red as a rosehip. 'So it is. It's a bella day.'

'Bella Day!' he laughed. Seemed tae find me funny. 'Is warm. Today. Like home. Mia home. Faraway,' he said. 'Italia. Lontano. Faraway.'

'Aye,' I says, still pickin the rosehips, and fillin up ma poke. Italia meant Italy, I thocht – the place that looked like a high-heeled boot on the maps at the school.

'You like potato? I dig in field. I cook. Tattie. Buono! Good!'

It wis ma turn tae laugh, the way he said it – 'tattie'. 'Aye,' I says, 'I suppose they're alright – tatties. Are you a prisoner? Yin o thae POWs doon in Robinsland Farm?'

'Si, si. My name Raffaello. Raffaello Lenati. You?'

'Mary – Mary Whyte.' It soonded awfie plain.

'Ah, Maria! Bella. Maria, you are my Bella Day!'

Maria – noo, yon was mair like it! He wis that bonnie. I couldnae concentrate on ma rosehip pickin for thinkin aboot his smile, and his easy laugh. I aye thocht tatties were just pasty plain, but see in his sun-tanned hands, when each bite slipped atween his white teeth, thae tatties looked like ambrosia, creamy and sweet. I made shair I went for rosehips every day.

There wis fair a buzz in the village aboot the POWs doon at Robinsland Farm. Specially ower Raffi and his pal Mr Cellani. They were hard workers, and nice natured. Ye could aye hear them singin their Italian sangs, fillin every note wi their herts. And they liked their tatties – a treat for them, they said. They dinnae eat tatties in Italy. It wis spaghetti back hame for them – *pasta*. Folk liked Cellani and Lenati. The bairns at the school made up a skippin rhyme aboot them. You could hear them singin it in the playground at dinner time:

> *Cellani and Lenati,*
> *braw Italianati,*
> *POWs*
> *doon in Robinsland Farm.*

> *Cellani and Lenati,*
> *nae mair spaghatti,*
> *they miss their Tally grub*
> *doon in Robinsland Farm.*

> *Cellani and Lenati*
> *are diggin the potati,*
> *they're fryin up chips*
> *doon in Robinsland Farm!*

Miss MacPhail aye comes oot the back shop like a slater frae under a stane. I'm shair the weather turned her grey the day she wis born. She's never liked me, nae maiter how hard I tried. She wis aye lookin tae pick on me, and she kent somethin wis up every dinnertime, when I left the shop wi a spring in ma step.

'You'll be down the Deanfoot Road again today, Mary, I take it?' she says yin mornin. She'd been burnin tae say somethin aa week. 'Your bag wasn't very full yesterday. Nor the day before. I know fine what you're up to down there at dinnertime.'

I telt her it wis takkin mair time tae find the rosehips, wi it gettin late in the season.

'Rosehips!' She very near spat at me. 'Is that your code name for those filthy Catholic foreigners! Fascisti. That's what they are, Mary. And all the silly skirts in Linton have been swinging down there since the sad day those parasites arrived.'

Silly skirts? She just said that cause naebody'd want tae look at whit's under hers. And anyway, Raffi's a gentleman. Milly MacPhail's the yin wi the dirty mind. I kent Raffi wis the enemy. I kent that fine. But noo he wis at Robinsland, he wis yin o us. He carved me a bonny wee cross wi rosehips on it. Gave it tae me.

'For Maria,' he said. 'For ma Bella Day.'

She wis fair in a flap yin mornin, Miss MacPhail. She'd been asked for cardboard boxes, and she telt me tae empty them aa in the back shop. I wis tae wrap the full stock o linen in tissue – towels, semmits, stockins – and fill up the drawers under the coonter.

'There's going to be no space in those drawers, no space at all,' she girned. 'And next thing we know they'll be wanting all my linen for bandages. There'll be nothing left to sell.'

'Whit's the boxes for, Miss MacPhail?'

'For the sphagnum moss. They're collecting it on the moor. Dressings for the wounded.'

'Moss? For dressins?'

'Nature's antiseptic,' she snaps, like I'm the Dunce o Deanfoot no tae ken. 'Now get cracking with those boxes, will you!'

Moss. I ken aa aboot moss. I ken the moors like the back o ma hand, aa the different moss ye can find, where it grows, saft when it's under ye, on a warm summer's day, up at the Kips, or roon by Mendick Hill. And doon at Robinsland.

I wis upstairs in bed at hame, middle o the nicht, and I heard this ringin ootside ma windae, like the bell o a bike. I got up, and liftit a corner o the blackoot felt. A beam o licht wis shinin up intae ma face frae the lane, blindin me. I couldnae tell who it wis, till the moon slipped oot frae under a clood, and washed its licht ower his face. Ma hert louped intae ma mooth. Raffi wis holdin his bike lamp.

'Maria!' he whispers. 'Maria. Bella Day!'

'Raffi! For God's sake!'

'Ssshhh!' he says, pittin his finger tae his lips. 'Is secret visit. Like Romeo and Giulietta!'

'If ma Grandad sees ye, I'll get the belt! And pit yer lamp oot. If the warden comes roon, he'll caa the polis!'

'Bella Day! Come down in la bella notte with me!'

'Whit?'

'Is beautiful night! Come!'

His eyes had yon look o far awa places. No like ma Dad. Ma Dad has eyes that nail ye, sae close and cauld they can kill. And red fists, like the lumps o meat he hacks wi a knife at Armstrong's Butchers. He'd gone tae the war – he couldnae wait tae get there, wherever it wis, and I reckon that wis the place for him. But no for Raffi. Raffi wisnae born for killin. He wis aye carvin somethin bonny oot o wood in his spare time at Robinsland, aye had a wee figure on the go.

I stood on the landin. I could hear ma Grandad snorin his heid aff. He couldnae get up in a hurry, wi his stump o a leg – had tae strap his tin yin on first, afore he could mak a move. And naethin ever wakened ma Mum yince she'd hit the hay. I pit a coat ower ma nightie, slipped intae ma welly boots, and sneaked oot the hoose, doon the steps tae the lane.

'Mia cara,' said Raffi, giein me a kiss. 'I take you on my bike.'

Efter that, he would come for me whenever the moon wis

up and the sky clear. We'd cycle doon tae Robinsland, me on the handlebars, and we'd sneak intae the barn. He'd mak a bed for us, wi his army coat and an auld blanket spreid ower the hay. The munitions trains were chuggin awa up on the moor. Sometimes the sirens would stairt tae wail, and then we'd hear planes goin ower. There wis a shelter up at the School Brae, but we couldnae be seen there thegither, in the middle o the nicht. We just lay in the barn, ticht in each ither's airms, hopin fur the best. At first licht, I'd creep awa, back hame.

I wis workin in MacFarlane's Drapers yin mornin, and Mrs Dodd came in for some net curtain.

'A yard and a half, please, Mary,' she says, lookin at me, her eyes like pins. 'Where's Miss MacPhail?'

'She's in the back shop,' I says, unrollin the net.

'Here,' says Mrs Dodd, pittin a broon poke on the coonter. 'Give her these, will you?'

'Right-oh,' I says, measurin oot the net.

'It's the parsnips she was asking for. She wants to boil them up with lemonade, to do as bananas.'

'Oh, aye.' And noo I'm cuttin the net. 'I heard o that. Never tried it. Does it work?'

'A Ministry of Food recipe. Works a treat,' says Mrs Dodd. 'My, you've gone a funny colour, Mary. Are you feeling alright?'

The thocht o parsnips swimmin aboot in lemonade suddenly turned ma stomach. I had tae stop cuttin the curtain, and I rushed intae the back shop. I hadnae time tae shut the lavvy door. Miss MacPhail stood watchin me while I threw up.

The next time it happened, I managed tae close the door. But I kent Miss MacPhail wis on the ither side, ready tae flay me wi her tongue.

'That's the second time you've been sick in the back shop this week, Mary, leaving a customer high and dry. It's a good skelp you're needing, if you ask me. Or sent to the minister. A dose of the scripture from Mr. Fraser would do no harm.'

The third time it happened, that wis it. She fair let rip:

'I'm not having this filthy carry-on rubbing off on MacFarlane's Drapers. Our boys are out there, getting killed to keep your freedom, and the good folk of Linton doing their bit for the war effort. But you, Mary Whyte? Down there at Robinsland, collaborating with the enemy! Well, I don't want to watch your dirty skirt getting tighter by the day. Find yourself a job some place else!'

I had tae tell Raffi. The kirk, wi its bonny carvin – that would be the place. It's aye open, for folk tae drap by. He came for me that nicht, on his bike. I telt him we werenae goin tae Robinsland till we'd been some place else first. We cycled doon tae the village green, and he leaned his bike by the graveyaird gate.

'Bring yer lamp,' I said.

Moonlicht wis streamin through the high windaes, as we stepped intae the kirk. The air wis chill and quiet.

'It isnae Catholic, but it's bonnie,' I whispered. Funny how ye aye whisper in a kirk. 'See,' I says, pointin tae the gallery, 'shine yer bike lamp.'

'Oh, Maria. Is bella! Look, the – how you say – leaves?'

'Ivy.'

'All wood!' He wis fair impressed.

'Aye. The border wi the thistles, there, roon the gallery, minded me o the rosehips ye carved for me on the wee cross. I kent ye'd like it! It wis twa ladies done it aa. Carved every bit.'

His eyes were shinin, fair lit up wi the miracle o the wooden vines.

'See this,' I said, takkin the lamp tae show him, 'the writin frae the bible, and the weepin willows carved roond it.'

Aa o a sudden, he sank doon next tae the font, his hale body heavin, hands ower his face. 'Sorry, Maria, sorry. I home sick. Italia.'

I'd never seen a man cry afore. They dinnae dae that here. I pit ma airms aroon him. 'Dinnae greet, Raffie. Dinnae. I've somethin tae tell ye. Listen. We're gonnie hae a bairn.'

He went quiet, didnae speak, just looked at me, like I was holy or somethin.

'Aye,' I says, 'A bairn, a… bambino. It's guid, no? Bene?'

He smiled then, and hugged me. 'Bene, Bella Day. Bene. Multo bene.'

Next mornin, ma Mum's gettin her coat on, tae go up tae the school, where she cooks in the kitchen. 'Ye're late reddin up the fire this mornin, Mary,' she says. 'Are ye no workin at MacFarlane's the day?'

I wis kneelin at the hearth, cleanin oot the grate, ma hands clarty wi ashes. I couldnae think whit way tae tell her, so I went through tae the kitchen tae gie masel time.

'Answer yer mither when she's talkin tae ye,' ma Grandad croaks frae the big airm chair, fed up cause his fire's no lit.

I had tae tell them. Ma Grandad went daft. Got up, and heezed himsel on his tin leg tae the sideboard. 'I'll leather ye for this!' he shouted, and yanked ma Dad's belt oot the drawer. 'Ye'll no feel the hide on yer erse when I've finished wi ye! Tae think I wis fechtin in thae trenches, knee deep in mud and guts, lossin a leg and earnin ma medals for *this*!' he yelled, layin intae me.

I wis sent awa, tae a boardin hoose near Lanark. Ma Grandad wis gonnie have tae pay for it oot his bit war pension. I wis tae stay there till I had ma bairn, and then gie it up for adoption.

I tried tae argue, but they wouldnae listen. 'Naebody'll ken till it stairts tae show,' I said. 'Can I no wait till efter Christmas?' I didnae want tae be awa frae Raffi sae lang. It wis only October, and ma bairn wisnae due till the beginnin o June. But the disgrace wis mair nor ma mither could bear.

'The hale o Linton kens ye've been doon at Robinsland every dinner time. And noo ye've been sacked, they'll aa jalouse why,' she says, ringin her hands. 'Mrs Dodd wis askin, only yesterday. 'I haven't seen Mary in MacFarlane's for a wee while. Is she no feelin weel?' Nosey bitch.'

Ma mither couldnae speak aboot it wioot greetin, and ma Grandad hirpled oot whenever I came intae the room.

'We'll say it's relations ye're goin tae stay wi, and ye've got a guid job there,' she says, her voice shakin, tears brimmin. 'That's whit we'll say.'

I wis packin ma case in ma bedroom, just aboot tae fold Raffi's wee rosehip cross intae ma nightie, when Mum comes in.

'Whit the hell's that?' she gasps, like she's seen the deil himsel. 'It's no enough ye're gonnae hae a Fascist bairn – ye're turnin Catholic on us noo!'

She grabbed the cross and ran doon stairs wi it. I tore efter her, shoutin, 'It's just a bit o carvin he gied me. I want tae keep it!'

'It can burn in hell, like you and yer bairn and yer Tally fancy man, for aa I care,' she screams, chokin wi tears as she chucked it in the fire I'd lit that mornin.

I watched the rosehips turn frae orange tae red and then tae black.

'Och, Mary,' sobbed ma Mum, clingin tae me, 'ye hae tae cut yer losses, lass. Cut them clean.'

I walked doon tae Robinsland tae say goodbye. It wis late autumn, and the wet smell o summer's wecht was in the moss and the gustin leaves. I hadnae seen much o Raffi since I telt him I wis bein sent awa, and had tae gie up oor bairn. We were baith prisoners o war, he'd said. I couldnae bring masel tae tell him aboot the cross, just couldnae find the words. The POWs and the landgirls were on their dinner break, and Raffi took me intae the barn. We sat doon in the hay.

'Maria,' he said, 'I make this for you.' And he gave me a wee boat, wi the name Bella Day carved on the side. 'Barchetta,' he says. 'Is for carry our amor, like the bambino.'

I pit it in ma pooch, and it stayed there.

At the boardin hoose, there were a few lassies waitin tae have their bairns. There wis yin, though, who'd had hers, and she wis holdin it, happed in a shawl, in the hallway, when I arrived.

The wumman in charge wis Myra Rankin. She looked like a teacher, wi her zipped up face. 'Right, Mary,' she says, yince I'd settled intae ma room. 'There's a load of washing waiting to be done, and the toilets are due to be cleaned. This isn't a rest home, and anyway, it's best to be active. Keeps you healthy until your baby's born. Nelly here will show you the ropes.' And then she left us alane. Nelly wis a quiet, weel-spoken lass, her belly big wi bairn. She gied me a basket o crumpled sheets, some o them stained, and took me tae the wash hoose. Sweat wis soon streamin doon our cheeks, as we rubbed the sheets in a haze o steam and carbolic.

'We're treated like slaves here, you know, and our parents have to pay for the privilege,' says Nelly, under her breath, in case Myra Rankin's listenin.

I wis used tae cleanin, so it didnae bother me. 'My mum says we're lucky to have someone that'll take us,' I says. 'Are you havin yer baby adopted?'

'Of course,' says Nelly, like it's a daft question. 'There's no choice. I'm dreading it, though. You're allowed to keep your baby for a while, mind you, to feed it yourself, so it gets a good start. But then you have to give it up.'

There wis a nice midwife came in sometimes, tae check yer bairn wis growin. She'd listen tae its hertbeat wi a metal horn, like ice on yer belly, but her hands were warm, and she never flyted me for no bein mairried. She aye said somethin tae keep yer spirits up. Nelly wis feart the people that adopted her bairn wouldnae be able tae love it, but the midwife telt her no tae worry. 'Bairns bring their love wi them,' she said. I liked that. She would come when a lassie was in labour, tae deliver the bairn. Ye'd hear the screamin frae the labour room, maistly in the middle o the nicht. I think it wis fear that made them cry oot – like wild animals they were. I wisnae feart. This wis Raffi's bairn inside me, an everythin aboot it wis richt.

A sleepy mill lade sloomed through the gairden. I'd be oot there first thing in the mornin, afore breakfast, if the weather wis nice, when it wis a 'bella day'. I'd tak Raffi's barchetta, the wee wooden boat, and float it on the watter, push it aboot wi a stick. Gied me a feelin o peace.

There wis an air raid shelter in the gairden, dug intae the ground, and when the siren went, we had tae get intae it. Sometimes, if there were a lot o lassies at the boardin hoose, we were packed ticht, and the new bairns would be in there wi us, sookin at their mithers' briests.

Come Christmas, I wis beginnin tae show, and I wisnae allowed hame. I sent a caird tae Raffi – I made it in ma room oot o a bit paper and a pencil I found in the kitchen drawer. I spent ages drawin it – a picture o his Bella Day boat, floatin on the mill lade wi a bairn in it, like Moses in the basket. I drew bullrushes in the watter an aa. I asked Myra Rankin for an envelope, and a stamp, thinkin she'll never say 'Yes,' but she did, and I wrote the boardin hoose address inside. I wisnae shair how tae spell

Raffi's name in the proper Italian, but it reached him, cause he sent me a letter back, his hand-writin fine, like his carvin, the words just how he spoke, in his ain Tally Scots I loved tae hear. And I could – I could hear him sayin every word I wis readin. He liked ma picture – *disegno*. He telt me no tae lose the barchetta, tae keep it safe. He wis waitin for me, he promised. The war would soon be ower, and he would tak me tae Italia. We would hae anither bambino, he said, if we couldnae keep this yin. 'But we're keepin it,' I telt masel. 'We're keepin it.'

I didnae get stamps as often as I liked, but I wrote a few letters tae Raffi, and he wrote a hale sheaf o them tae me. Mrs Grieg at Robinsland wis a guid wumman, and gied him the paper and stamps when he asked.

The snawdraps had passed, and the crocuses were pushin through. Ma belly wis gettin bigger. I wisnae sleepin weel, and I wis tired aa the time. This nichtmare kept comin at me. It got sae bad I wis feart tae shut ma eyes when I hit the pillow. I had a bairn in ma dream, a wee lassie, tiny and perfect in every way. Only, in this nichtmare, I'd forget aboot her for days on end – forget tae feed and change her. Then, o a sudden, I'd mind, and I'd rush tae ma room, and she'd be there, in her cot, quiet as a moose, lookin up at me wi patient eyes, Raffi's eyes, big and broon. Her cheek and jaw banes were cutting through her face like a skull. She was stairvin. Her skin was yellow, and the cot wis aa stained wi a terrible liquid, cause I hadnae changed her. I'd forgotten tae look efter her. How could I forget tae look efter ma ain bairn? But she wis still alive, and pleased tae see me in her quiet way, and I wis greetin, and greetin, as I cleaned her up and pit her tae ma briest. The milk rushed oot intae her face, and her mooth tried tae catch it, but she wis that hungry she was chokin. And then I'd wake up.

I took tae cairryin the barchetta aboot wi me everywhere, in ma pinnie pooch, and under ma pillow at nicht. I tried tae imagine ma heid inside the Bella Day, like the boat was a helmet against the nichtmare. Sometimes it worked.

'Ne'er cast a cloot till May is oot,' ma mither used tae say. I aye supposed she meant the month. 'No, no,' says Myra Rankin, aye correctin me. 'It's the hawthorn that's being referred to.' Weel, the month had come roon, and wi it, the hawthorn, bloomin like white brides aa ower the fields and roadsides, as weel's the yellow broom. The weather was warm, and I wis castin ma cloots aa the time, wearin a cotton dress and nae vest. But I aye wore ma pinnie.

The wireless wis on in the kitchen yon day we heard the news we'd aa been waitin for.

'Will you listen to that!' says Miss Rankin, pittin doon her cup o tea. 'Glory be to God, the war's over. Like the song says: 'Tomorrow, when the world is free.' And here we are, Mary: tomorrow is today!'

I said nothin, just paused for a moment, and then cairried on wi ma moppin.

'Have you nothing to say, girl?' she says. 'No, I don't suppose you'd understand the real meaning of freedom, would you, with your loose morals and your selfish ways.'

And that wis it. I stopped moppin, picked up the bucket, chucked the hale load o dirty watter at her, and ran oot the hoose. And I kent the meanin o' freedom, I'm tellin ye, as I ran doon the road, ma bairn in ma belly, and naebody tellin me whit tae dae. I got tae a crossroads, and I seen an army truck comin by. I flagged it doon.

'That's some bump on you, girlie!' laughed a soldier laddie, as they drew up aside me. 'Are you needin the hospital?'

'No yet,' I says, 'but I'm needin a lift. Whaur are ye heided?'

'For Leith.'

'That'll dae,' I says.

'Hop in!'

'The War's ower,' I telt them, as they pulled me up intae the truck. 'I just heard it on the wireless.'

'It's official, lads!' cries the soldier next tae me. They aa stairtit tae cheer, and then burst intae sang, wi *The White Cliffs o Dover*, changin the words, singin: 'Today, now the world is free!'

We were drivin through the moors, up the Lang Whang, and they were still giein it laldy. I could see the Pentlands comin closer. The weather wis douce and warm, and I wondered if Raffi would still be at Robinsland. I dozed in the heat o the truck.

'Where are we?' I says, suddenly awake.

'We're near somewhere called Balerno, darlin,' said the driver, a cheery Englishman.

'Balerno?! Aaready? Ye'd better let me get doon.'

We waved goodbye, and I watched them drive aff up the brae. There wisnae a single clood in the wide blue sky, and I could hear a whaup's cry bubblin ower the moor.

I walked up intae the Pentlands, on the Monk's Path frae Balerno tae Nine-Mile-Burn. I dipped the barchetta in a burn and drank the sweet, peaty watter. The gorse wis a fierce yellow, shinin in the sun, and smellin like the coconuts ye win at the shows. I lay doon in the moss, and felt the warmth o the moor seep intae ma hale body.

When I came to, the sun had set, and the gloamin wis creepin ower the saddle o the Kips. There wis a chill in the air. I had naethin on but ma thin cotton dress, and ma pinnie. I should hae grabbed a cast aff cloot afore leavin, if I'd had the time tae think. I got up and I kept goin.

A skelf o moon wis risin in the sky when I felt the first pain. I sat doon on a stane, and a flood o watter rushed atween ma legs. I've got tae get tae Nine-Mile-Burn afore the bairn comes, I telt masel. I walked on, and efter a bit, the pains stopped. I washed masel clean in Logan Burn, then swung doon below the Kips.

I wis just passin the stane whaur the monks' cross used tae staun, when a wave o pain owertook me, and I had tae stop. The bairn's comin, I thocht, and it willnae wait. I hunkered doon on aa fowers, gruppin ontae the stane. I heard masel scraikin. I couldnae haud back the soond that wis rippin oot ma throat. I could feel the bairn's heid pushin doon, and I wisnae shair whit tae dae. The river o pain just kept buckin through me. Oot o naewhaur, a dug's tongue wis lickin ma face, and a shepherd wis bent ower me.

'Ye're daein fine, lass,' he says, 'ye're daein fine.'

I stairtit tae greet like I'd never stop.

'Aye, aye, you greet, lass, that's it, you greet,' he says, gien ma belly a pat, 'I'm gonnae hae tae pit ma haund inside ye – the cord's mibbe wrapped roon the bairn's neck. We'll hae tae gie it a bit help.'

She wis limp and grey as a stane in the shepherd's airms. A dreidfu colour, no richt at aa. He cut the cord, tied it, pit her doon on his jaiket, and rubbed her aa ower, blawin intae her mooth tae gie her braith. 'Come on, come on, ma bairnie,' I heard him mutter through his teeth, intae her skin, pressin and rubbin the cage o her wee chest, willin her no tae gie up. Then her eyelids fluttered like twa tiny moths, and she gied a stutter o life.

'Aye, aye, that's it, she's comin back,' he says, 'she's comin back.'

I stayed wi the shepherd and his faimily for a while. Soon as I wis weel enough, I went tae Robinsland, cairryin ma bairn, doon the Deanfoot Road. I'd heard aa the POWs had gone. Mrs Grieg telt me Raffi and Mr Cellani had left a fortnicht syne. She missed them. It wis quiet, she said, wioot their singin.

Dad's hame frae the war, aa in yin piece, but he disnae say much. He'll no hae me or the bairn in the hoose. Mum comes oot tae see us whaur we bide – anither big boardin hoose, a mansion, sittin in the hills, no far frae hame. I've got a room and a job there, cleanin again. Yin o the ladies wha carved the bonnie wood in the kirk lived there, lang syne, but it's been empty for years. Till a gairdener frae Austria came. He wis like a missionary or somethin, lookin fur a hame for bairns that naebody wants tae look efter. Some o the bairns cannae speak. Some o them never will, and maist o them hae a farawa look in their eyes. I like it here. The folk work hard. They're Christian, though they're no Catholic or Protestant. I'm no shair whit they are, but nae maiter – suits me fine. The gairdener plays the fiddle for the dancin and singin, and we laugh a lot. There's a lass frae Germany – a refugee. She's hud a bairn frae a soldier that went tae the war and didnae come back. She wisnae married, same as me. But naebody bothers aboot that kind o thing here.

Mum came oot the ither day, wi a letter for me. I didnae ken the handwritin – no Raffi's. It wis frae his friend, Mr Cellani, aa written oot in gey guid English. They were in a truck, he said, him an Raffi, wi a crowd o POWs, headin hame through the north o France. They'd stopped on the road, tae gie their legs a stretch. Raffi seen a bit wood lyin in a field that he fancied for carvin. He'd been quiet aa mornin, and Cellani asked him how he wis feelin. Raffi said he was thinkin aboot his Maria, and he was shair oor bairn must be on its way. Carvin a bit wood aye gied him peace, and he walked intae the field. Cellani saw it, the moment it happened: Raffi stepped on a land mine, and that was it.

He'd tried tae stay on at Robinsland – he wanted tae mairry

me, and keep the bairn. He'd asked the minister, the army, and the police. The fermer wis mair than willin tae keep Raffi on, Cellani said – he wis that weel liked, but it wasnae allowed. POWs couldnae stay.

I walked intae Linton wi ma bairn last nicht, cairryin her on ma hip, in a blanket sling. It's midsummer, and the gloamin's late. We passed under Mendick Hill, by the hoose where I wis born, and took the path ower the Roman Bridge. I used tae mak camp fires there as a bairn. We crossed the village green tae the burn. I dipped Raffi's barchetta intae it, and cairried the watter tae the kirk, wioot spillin a drap.

Aa wis still and quiet. I unwrapped the blanket and held her ower the font. I mindit ma mither tellin me aboot it, the font – some lads found it in the burn, efter the Great War, pulled it oot in bits, broken, but the mason pit it back thegither. I poured the watter ower her heid.

She didnae greet at the cauld splash, just blinked and looked up at me wi Raffi's dark eyes. The doctor says she's no richt, no enough oxygen wi the cord roond her neck.

'But ye're mine' I telt her, giein her broo anither wee jaup o haly watter, for guid luck. 'I name you Bella Day.'

# Letting Go

LILY SAT IN the lee of Neidpath Castle, above the River Tweed. She'd been looking forward to this – a day out with her daughter in one of her favourite places. She lived only a few miles away, but a long illness had kept her indoors, and she hadn't been here for years. Gean blossoms spread a canopy from the roadside gate all the way to the castle, and the daffodils were in full bloom. Snug in her wheelchair, Lily patted the rug on her knees.

High above, on the grey whinstone battlements, doves crooned – *cooshie-doos*, Jean called them. The sound made Lily feel – what was that word? *Lown* – peaceful. The air was *douce* on her paper-thin skin. Another good word. Just right for a light Spring breeze that's been exiled all winter. Scots words she'd come to love and use, second nature now.

'You alright, Mum?' asked Jean, adjusting the wheelchair on uneven ground. 'Warm enough?'

'Don't fuss. I'm fine.'

The Tweed flowed south to England. 'I wouldn't be here but for the Border,' Lily thought, her mind meandering down the years to a bedroom window that looked onto a cobbled Lancashire street – last year at high school just after the War, and her class mates were calling up to her:

'Come on down, Lil! We're going for a picnic by the canal!'

But her mother wouldn't let her: 'I know who'll be there

– Harry Carter, bloody traitor, out of prison and livin it up. You're havin nowt to do wi him, that coward conchie. Too frit to serve his country.'

Lily watched her friends laughing away along the street without her. The same window she'd stood at, a few years before, shivering in her nightie, the midnight horizon an inferno – Manchester on fire.

'A penny for them, Mum?'

'War.'

'What – on a day like today? You need a cuppa! I've got a flask here in my bag.'

The tea slipped down Lily's throat, warm and sweet.

'Shame they've never finished restoring old Neidpath,' said Jean, looking up at the ruined wing of the tower.

'Cromwell,' replied Lily.

'What about him?'

'He hit it. Or his soldiers did.' Lily took another sip, relishing the topic as much as the tea. History, filling in the gaps. 'Over in minutes, some say. Others have it down as days.'

'Well, it can hardly be both,' said Jean, topping up her mother's cup.

'Oh, yes it can! Always two sides to a story. Edward the First – a great statesman where I come from. But here, he's Hammer of the Scots.'

'And what do *you* think?' asked Jean. Her mother was on a roll, and she was glad to see it, that old fire sparking.

'Well, he hammered the lord of this place – what's his name…' Lily screwed up her eyes, rummaging through her mind. 'Sheriff of Peebles… Fraser. That's it. Had him packed off to London, and chopped to bits, same as Wallace.'

Jean looked up at the castle. 'I come from here, and I didn't know that.'

Lily shook her head. 'Edward was a right baddun!'

'Listen to you! They'll be calling you a traitor!'

'Too late. I'm that already,' said Lily, handing back her empty cup.

'Will we take a wander round the corner?' asked Jean. 'Get another view?'

'Alright. But watch you don't have me toppling down the brae – it's steep!'

The wheelchair bumped over rough ground to the castle's north side, where Jean stopped suddenly, and put on the brake. 'Och!' she tutted. 'I thought we might see the viaduct from here, but I always forget it's hidden round that bend in the river.'

'Doesn't matter. I've got the picture in *here*.' Lily tapped her forehead. 'We took a trip over it once, your Dad and me, just before it closed. The Caledonian Railway.' She shut her eyes – could see them now, sixty-odd years ago, the two of them carried over those graceful arches, the Tweed sweeping beneath them through lush green hills. Harry squeezed her hand. He knew what was at stake. She could still feel the mixture of elation and dread, their boldness – leaving home and getting married, without her parents' consent. The finality. Her mother's threat still rang in her ears: 'If you wed that coward conchie we'll have nowt to do wi you ever again!'

'You can throw me ashes from the viaduct, Jean – be a fine place!'

'Oh, for goodness' sake, Mum! I don't want to think about *that*.'

'You're going to have to one day, and it can't be far off.'

'Well, I refuse to think about it right now. Not today.'

'Thought's no bad thing,' said Lily. 'Unless, of course, you think like *her*.'

'Who?'

'Me mother: "You know what *Thought* did? Followed a muck-cart and *thought* it were a weddin."'

Their laughter ricocheted off the castle walls. Gean blossoms drifted down the brae on the still air, petals landing on Lily's lap. *Gean.* Another good Scots word. Her parents' house, where she grew up, was called Cherry Trees. But she liked *gean* better. The right sound for that sharp flavour of the flame-coloured fruit – a wee stab of fire on the tongue and eye. 'How does the song go, Jean?' She tapped a rhythm impatiently on the arm of her wheelchair. 'The geans and John MacLean... la la la... come on – you must remember it!' She closed her eyes for a moment till it came to her:

> *When MacLean meets wi's freens in Springburn,*
> *A' the roses and geans will turn tae bloom,*
> *And a black boy frae yont Nayanga*
> *Dings the fell gallows o' the burghers doon.*

Jean looked slightly forlorn. 'You know more about Scotland than I do, Mum.'

Lily gave her a reassuring pat. 'You never needed her like I did. She gave me a grand bit of mothering when I was rock bottom. The least I could do was get to know her.'

It was blossom time that day at Cherry Trees, when she came home from school to find the house empty, a note on the mantelpiece – her mother's writing: *Gone to hospital to get a baby.* Get a baby? Didn't they somehow come from inside you? At nine years old, she wasn't quite sure. She'd never noticed her mother changing – always a big woman, broad and heavy, and Lily hadn't seen much of her lately, banished after school each day to the back room, where her parents had a dingy little corner shop.

'Go and stand at the counter for a bit!' her mother would shout from upstairs, the minute Lily came home. 'Dad's on late shift at mill, won't be back till ten.'

She liked the smell in there, the tang of newspapers and liquorice. And the ginger beer was so inviting, fizzing in the old stoneware bottles. She'd been doing it for weeks – pulling the corks out, and taking a sip or two from each one. Now and again, when she thought she might have overdone it, she'd get a jug of water from the kitchen, and top them up. You could tell by the weight if they weren't full, and the sound too, especially when she'd had a bit of a binge. The ginger beer would slosh about in the half-empty bottles with a thin kind of splish – a real give-away. And the customers had noticed.

'You're a right mean un, Jane Bartle,' they accused her mother. 'Mekkin it go further wi tap water! You should think shame!'

Lily got it in the neck. 'You're a traitor, a bloody traitor to our family name!' her mother shouted, once they'd gone, their money refunded. 'Our reputation's mud! It'll be a miracle if we have any custom at all, at this rate!'

'Give over, Jane,' her Dad had said. He was *douce*. A right soft un. 'She's only lickle – didn't mean nuthin by it.'

And now a baby sister. Clara. Lily loved her, in spite of the rocky start. Eyes like forget-me-nots, and blue ribbons to match, big bows tied into those thick blonde curls – not rat-brown straight like her own lank hair. And Clara's laughter, gold in that dark house. But things were worse than ever with her mother: 'Leave the babbie alone!' she'd snap, whenever Lily was dandling Clara on her knee. 'She's nowt to do wi you. Get behind that counter, and look after the shop!'

'Fancy a sweetie?'

'Where... what?' murmured Lily, surfacing.

Jean was opening a cellophane bag. 'You're in a dwam, Mum – miles away!' She held a small lime-green globe up to the sunlight. 'Here – have one.'

Lily sucked on the sweet sourness, and Jean gave her a playful dunt on the head. The kids used to love the story – lots of mock thumping when Gran brought out the Soor Plooms – named after English raiders who came over the Border, and got walloped by the Scots for snaffling their unripe plums. That was how she coped with the past – turned it into stories for her family's amusement. Have a laugh. The Border. Sour and sweet. She'd crossed it and lost her family, but made a new one – her own. Nearly a lifetime ago. Had Clara forgotten all those nights when she'd sneak into her big sister's bed, asking for stories? But nothing, no reply to her letters and the photos she'd sent – young Jean, being crowned Queen of the Beltane Festival; another of her graduation; then her first job, PE teacher in Kelso; and that favourite, years later, of John, Jean's lad, riding in the Beltane Bell race – 'Freedom!' he'd shouted, acting the daft bloke as he crossed the finishing line to win the silver trophy.

Lily longed to share these moments with her sister. When she held Jean for the first time, she was lost. Those blue eyes, just like Clara's – looking into them made her feel she was being swallowed up in a vast, empty sky. For days she felt utterly forsaken. But Harry took them for a walk up a hill – May, it was, bees buzzing in the yellow whins, a *braw* day, like a ballad. He spread his coat for her on the grass, in that way of his – no fuss. She sat down on it, leaned her back against an old dry-stane dyke, and put Jean to her breast. The Tweed shone like a ribbon below. A sudden clatter cracked the air, as a torrent of horses forded the water. The riders' whoops rang with the hooves, the standard bearer's colours flying in the breeze – her first sight of the Beltane Ride Out.

Back at the house, neighbours came round with soup and sandwiches, and the young midwife dropped by again. 'Would you just look at the twa o ye,' she'd said, seeing Jean at Lily's breast. 'Ye're juist made for each ither!'

A vote of confidence, a lifeline she needed right then, thrown to her by that young woman. Lily was sure that's what got her into nursing. The National Health Service, her badge of honour. Better than a drab corner shop any day.

'Mum!'

She opened her eyes to see Jean waving at her from down the brae, clambering back up, with a handful of daffodils. 'Did you have a nice snooze in the sun?'

'Daydreaming – of you coming into the world. You looked just like Clara. Still do.'

Jean placed the flowers on her mother's lap. 'Time to go home. Dad'll be wondering where we've got to.'

'I wish…'

'What?'

But Lily couldn't say it.

'Tell me, Mum. What?'

'I wish that… that we'd talked. Me and Clara. I wish she'd answer my letters. I wish she'd come and visit – meet you…your family… I miss her, I've missed her my whole life.' It was all tumbling out now – no jokes, no stories – like a river in spate.

Jean took an envelope from her pocket. 'We weren't sure if we should show you this, Dad and me. It came in the post. I've had it in my jacket for days.'

It was from Lancashire, sent by a neighbour, with a cutting from a local newspaper – Clara's death notice – and an accompanying letter. She'd never married. Ran the family shop all her days, till recently, when she'd died in a nursing home, which had just been closed down.

Lily and Jean watched in silence as the sun dipped below Neidpath's battlements. A sudden gust snatched the cutting from Lily's bird-frail hand. It fluttered off down the brae, and Jean made to chase after it, but Lily tugged at her sleeve: 'Let it go.'

'Don't you want it for keeping?'

'No. Let the river take it.'

Jean turned the wheelchair round, and pushed her mother slowly along the path, under the geans. 'You alright, Mum?'

'I'm douce,' she said quietly. 'Lown.'

And she was.

# Colour

KIRSTY HAD NEVER met a black person till she was seven. The first time was at Waverley Station.

They took the bus into Edinburgh – Kirsty, her Mum and wee sister Peggy – with a present for Paul Robeson. Dad wanted to be there too, but they wouldn't let him away from his work at the school. There was a big crowd. Mum spoke to a policeman and he helped them to the front. Then there was a bang, and Kirsty thought they'd been shot. But Mum said it was only the One o'Clock Gun fired from the castle. Next thing, Paul Robeson stepped off the train. Tall and dark, he towered over everyone. The son of an escaped slave, Dad had told her. His smile was so bright Kirsty thought she could feel its heat on her cold cheeks. She'd never seen a smile like that before.

Mum fished about in her shoulder bag with one hand, gripping Peggy at her hip with the other. 'Here we are, Kirsty,' she whispered, pulling out a big brown envelope. 'You give it to him – go on!'

Kirsty stepped forward in her prickly tartan skirt.

'Is this for me?' asked Paul Robeson, bending over her. He wasn't singing, but she recognised his deep voice from Dad's records the moment he spoke. She couldn't think what to say – her words got stuck. She looked up to Mum for help.

'It's a song, Mr Robeson,' said Mum, her cheeks going all pink. 'A gift. From my husband – he's a composer.'

He thanked her, and sat down on a bench, lifting Kirsty and Peggy onto his knees. Cameras popped and clicked all around.

The second time, it was another musician – Dad's friend from Ghana. Kirsty waited with Dad to meet him at the bus stop. He stepped down onto the grey pavement like a sunbeam in his long yellow robes and golden cap.

'Your little daughter!' he laughed, and swept her into a blaze of cloth that smelled like coconuts and cinnamon toast. Then he walked with them all the way down the village street, like the King of Africa, holding her hand.

So when Mum and Dad said the family would be moving to Cape Town, Kirsty was over the moon. But her brother Calum wasn't. He was the oldest, about to go to high school and wanted to stay in Scotland with his friends.

'You'll make new friends at your new school,' Kirsty told him. 'Black friends!'

'What's that got to do with anything?' Calum grumped. 'I just want the ones I've got here.'

There weren't any black people on the big lilac ship that carried them over the Atlantic from Southampton. The luxury amazed Kirsty, even though they were only travelling Tourist Class, according to Mum – First Class was too expensive, she said. But still! A cinema, shops, playroom, library, and up on deck, a squash court and swimming pool. Kirsty felt like a princess in the cabin she shared with Mum and Peggy, pink roses all over the wallpaper, with matching rosy sheets, pillowcases and bedspreads. Calum and Dad were next door, their room done up in a lovely shade of bluey green – 'aquamarine' Mum called it. Meals were served by silver-buttoned waiters in the long, wide dining room. Calum liked to collect the menus – food Kirsty had never heard of: *Baked Kingklip Caprice, Consomme Aurore, Savoury Croquette Napolitaine.*

'You know, Seamus, this is the first time you've relaxed in years,' Mum said to Dad, glad to see him up on deck in the sunshine, happy with his books. Kirsty had been worried about him back home in Scotland – sometimes he seemed very tired, and didn't always breathe properly. He'd been in hospital, but Mum and Dad didn't talk about it much. Calum seemed to know, though, and said it was something to do with his lungs – the South African sunshine was going to heal them. Dad had been working too hard, teaching in the school by day, and writing his music at night. The job at the university in Cape Town was going to give him more time for his own work, and he wouldn't get so tired.

'Where's the line, Mum?' Kirsty asked, looking out over the Atlantic. 'I thought there was a line.'

'There is,' said Mum, 'but it's invisible.'

The ship was crossing the Equator, and everyone had come out on deck for the big ceremony, all the children wearing their swimsuits. Kirsty's was new – she'd gone shopping for it with Mum to Jenners in Edinburgh before they left, and she loved it – bright purple, ruched and skirted, with gold polka dots.

A man roared at the crowd. Kirsty shuddered at the pink, fleshy chest and shoulders that flashed through his long beard and mane of yellow hair.

'That's Neptune,' said Dad, 'the sea-god.'

Mum seemed to find him funny: 'And that daft bit of plastic he's waving is his trident!'

'He looks like the ship's captain,' said Calum.

'Who's first for my briny bath?' bawled Neptune. Mermaids whooped and giggled beside him, as he dunked children, one at a time, in a huge barrel of water.

'Go on, Cal – it's your turn,' nudged Dad.

'No! No! Don't go!' screamed Peggy, clinging to Dad's neck.

Calum stepped up, shaking in his swimming trunks.

'Hold your nose, shrimp,' growled Neptune, 'and count to ten!'

Kirsty watched in horror as the hairy pink hand pushed Calum into the barrel and held him under for ages. But he came out alive. The crowd cheered. Then someone shoved her forward. She flapped and gulped in the sea-god's grip. Just when she thought she'd drowned, Neptune hauled her back up to the air, and Mum rushed in with towels.

'Look! There's Table Mountain!' Dad called to them. 'Devil's Peak on one side, and that's the Lion's Head on the other!'

Calum made a face. 'I like the Pentland Hills better.'

'What a reception we're getting!' said Mum, as the ship neared the harbour. A brass band was playing on the pier in the sunshine. The musicians were dressed in dazzling white, and next to them, in two long lines, soldiers stood to attention. 'They're welcoming the one millionth migrant from Britain to South Africa,' said Mum.

'Is that you, Dad?' asked Calum.

'Me?! No. It's for that man over there, the one talking to the captain.'

'We can pretend it's for us, though,' winked Mum.

A car was waiting to take them out of Cape Town to 'the suburbs', where they were going to rent a university staff house. The roadsides shimmered for miles with rainbow flowers.

The house had a veranda at the front – a *stoep*, it was called – where you could eat out, watching huge butterflies float by over the lawn. The kitchen window looked up to towering Devil's

Peak. Kirsty ran out to explore the back garden, and found a kind of concrete stable. Or maybe it was a kennel. 'Can we have a dog – or a horse?!' she shouted to Mum and Dad.

'That's your servant's quarters,' called a voice from the garden next door. Another family was watching them. 'Welcome!' smiled the father, a big man with a strong accent. 'Come and have a bite with us. You'll need something before you unpack!'

They sat at a table on the neighbours' stoep. Mr. De Groot asked for silence. His wife and four children crossed their hands on place mats. It took Kirsty a moment to realise what was happening. Mum nodded at her across the table to bow her head, and Calum almost choked, trying not to laugh. He always did that when he was embarrassed, which annoyed Kirsty, and she kicked him under the table. Mr. De Groot made a short speech in a language she didn't understand, though she recognised the word God. The moment he finished, his children were squawking like seagulls, reaching out for *mealies* – a kind of pale, creamy corn on the cob – served by a quiet black woman.

'More bread, Martha!' Mrs De Groot called to her above the racket, 'and bring some more lemonade. These Scotch kids have brought an appetite with them – *maak gou,* girl!'

Next morning there was a ring at the doorbell. Kirsty ran to answer it. A young black woman with no teeth stood on the stoep, asking if she could speak to 'Madam'.

'I'm sorry,' said Mum, when the young woman explained she was looking for work. 'Really – I am. It's just that we don't actually need a maid.'

Peggy came into the doorway, holding onto Kirsty's skirt. The young woman's long black fingers ruffled Peggy's fluffy blonde hair.

'I like children. I can help you, Madam.'

'I felt terrible, turning her away like that,' Mum said to Dad afterwards. 'She needs a job, I know. But we've always cleaned up our own dirt.'

There was a swimming pool across the road. *Whites Only,* announced the notice board at the entrance.

'What does that mean, Dad?' asked Calum.

'It means black people can't swim here.'

Kirsty was surprised. 'What – Paul Robeson can't swim with us if he comes to stay?'

'Don't be ridiculous, Kirsty!' said Mum. 'He won't be coming to stay.'

That wasn't the point, Kirsty thought. And anyway, he might visit if he liked Dad's song.

Guava trees grew in the garden, heavy with perfumed fruit. Kirsty found some brown paper bags in the kitchen, filled them up, and wrote on each one in felt-tipped pen: *Guavas – 5 cents – Blacks Only.* Then she placed them in a row on the garden wall overlooking the street pavement, sat Peggy next to them, and waited for customers. Mrs De Groot was the first.

'What are you doing, child?! This isn't a market! And blacks? You don't want to be touching their money – you don't know where it's been!' She grabbed the bags, carried them into the kitchen, and thumped them down on the table. 'You need to keep an eye on that daughter of yours,' she warned Mum.

Kirsty hardly ever saw black children anywhere, not even in town when she went shopping with Mum. They seemed to live somewhere else. And there were no black pupils at Springville Junior School. It was for white girls only – a sea of blue and white checked dresses, white ankle socks and hats called straw boaters. A black man, tall and bent, looked after the garden. Everyone called him *boy*, though he looked old enough to be Paul Robeson's father, Kirsty thought.

One of her new school friends gave her a box of silk worms. She needed mulberry leaves to feed them. The old gardener picked them for her from a mulberry tree that grew in the school grounds. She loved to lower her fingers into the box and feel the rhythm of the worms' sleek skins while they feasted.

'Look after them well and they'll spin cocoons,' the gardener told her. 'Sometimes you'll get different colours, not just white – like yellow and green – sometimes pink.'

Another girl who sat next to her in class gave her a chameleon. It lived among the flowerpots on a shelf at home. Kirsty liked to place it on different coloured surfaces, and watch its skin change to match the surroundings. 'Let's put it on your kilt and see if it turns tartan!' she said to Calum the day she brought it home.

'Don't be daft,' he snorted. 'You'll give the thing a heart attack!'

There were lots of parties – barbeques, called *braaie*, at friends' houses on wide green lawns under lilac clouds of jacaranda blossom, trips in a sports car with Dad's friend who owned a recording studio, and – Kirsty's favourite – the university film club, where she saw the girl *Gigi* become the most glamorous woman in Paris.

Calum wasn't happy, though. He was homesick. He'd make menus for the dinner table, like the ones they'd had on the ship, with drawings of places he missed, their names written underneath in fancy lettering: *The Moorfoot Hills on the Road to Peebles*, or *The Pentlands on a Winter Morning*. And he was always playing his Andy Stewart record, especially the song about a kilt:

*I've just come down from the Isle of Skye*
*I'm no very big and I'm awful shy,*
*the lassies shout when I go by:*
*'Donald where's yer troosers?'*

The African weather didn't suit him. He kept fainting in the heat, and Mum was anxious about him. Dad had heard about a Scottish Highland Show, and Calum was desperate to go.

'But how will we get there?' Mum wondered. 'It's miles away.'

All the families they knew in Cape Town had cars, but Mum and Dad didn't drive. Back in Scotland, hardly anyone owned a car in their village.

'We'll take a bus,' said Dad. 'It'll be fun to have a jaunt.'

It was just about cool enough for Calum to wear his kilt without melting. The field was a sea of tartan, crowds of people watching the competitions – Highland dancing, bagpipe and caber-tossing. Lunch was in a marquee – haggis burgers and Lorne sausage, and Mum was glad to see Calum really happy for once.

Peggy snoozed in Dad's arms on the bus journey home, and Calum read his souvenir programme. Kirsty watched the passengers' faces. Mum elbowed her in the ribs. 'Stop staring at people!'

But she couldn't help it. She'd become interested in skin colour, working out who was darkest, who was lightest – black, brown, white or in-between. Most of the passengers were black. She counted only nine white people, including her own family, and all the whites were sitting at the front. The thick pink of the driver's neck folding over his collar made her shiver. He must be white, she thought, like Neptune. But the bus conductor was an in-between – *Cape Coloured*, that shade was called.

A black man had got onto the bus at the last stop. He was wearing oily working clothes, and was arguing with the conductor.

'What's going on?' Mum asked Dad.

'Not sure – looks like he's lost something.'

'I've got a return ticket, *baas*. I bought it. I did!' said the black man, digging into all his pockets. 'It's somewhere here, I'm telling you.'

'Well, you'd better hand it over, or you're off the bus,' warned the conductor.

'I've got it – I have. Give me a minute, *baas*.'

'D'you think I'm a mug? You're trying to cadge a free ride.'

By now the bus had stopped. Everyone was watching.

The black man gave up on looking for his ticket, stared at the conductor and sneered: 'You're a coloured man – a *brak*, man, a *brak*.'

The blood drained from the conductor's face. 'Maybe he is white,' thought Kirsty. He grabbed the black man by his collar, said something to the driver, and the bus zoomed off. A few minutes later it stopped outside a police station, the engine still running. The conductor turned to the passengers:

'Who'll hold this *kaffir* for me, then, eh?'

A big man bustled forward, '*Ek sal! Ek sal!*' Kirsty could understand him. She was learning Afrikaans at school, her class marching round the desks with pretty Miss Povey, pretending to be soldiers holding guns, singing:

> *Met 'n boom-boom hier*
> *en 'n boom-boom daar,*
> *Hoeraaaa! Suid Afrika!*

From the way the big Afrikaner grabbed hold of the black man,

Kirsty thought there was going to be a fight. Dad was shaking, and got up to speak, Peggy clinging round his neck, but Mum pulled him down before he'd opened his mouth.

'Do you want the police in the house?!' she hissed.

An old white woman stood up behind them, every wrinkle on her face and neck quivering like her voice: 'Can't we just forget this? I'll pay for his ticket. Let's drive on.'

But the conductor was already inside the police station. The whole bus was hushed, only the hum of the engine, still running. The conductor came back with a policeman who shouted an order in Afrikaans. The black man was thrown down the steps of the bus by the big Afrikaner who'd been holding him. From the window Kirsty saw the policeman's high black boots flash in the evening sun as he kicked the black man again and again – across the road, through the gate, up the path and into the police station.

'He'll be lucky if he comes out with his teeth in,' said Mum, under her breath.

The bus moved off. Twilight shadowed everyone, and no-one spoke. Mum and Dad were upset, tears running down Mum's cheeks. Peggy's cries stabbed the silence. Kirsty felt the world had emptied. And she could see the longing in Calum's eyes.

Her silk worms had spun their cocoons, yellow, green and soft pink, like a pale rainbow, just as the gardener had said. They hatched in her room and flitted about the house, annoying Mum, who told her not to bring any more silk worms home, though she could keep her lovely cocoons. Kirsty still met up with the gardener at break time. She enjoyed their chats. At first he didn't say much, but over time she learned about his life in the township where he lived. He had a grandson who wanted to be a musician. But this wasn't likely, he told her, since they'd no money to send him to a college, not with his son on Robben Island, anyway.

'Where's that?' Kirsty asked.

'In Table Bay. It's a prison island.'

A prison island. It sounded like something in one of her Enid Blyton books. Scary and thrilling.

Christmas was near, and Calum kept fainting in the heat.

'Are we getting a tree?' Kirsty asked Mum.

'I don't think so. It doesn't seem right without snow.'

They went to the beach on Christmas Day. Dad decided to hire a taxi. Mum thought it would be too expensive, but Dad wanted to give them all a treat. 'And anyway,' he said, 'no point in spoiling things again with public transport.'

Mum packed a picnic hamper. Everything was tartan – the napkins, paper cups and plates, and crackers with tartan crowns falling out when you pulled them. To cheer up Calum – Kirsty knew it. The beach was busy, and they had to walk a while before they found a quiet patch. The minute they'd settled, Peggy stripped off.

'I can't keep so much as a vest on this child,' Mum sighed, slapping sun cream all over the wee one's body. 'I've no sooner got her dressed than she's naked again!'

'She's a sun-worshipper!' laughed Dad, watching Peggy run off naked along the sand, a chicken leg gripped in her fat wee fist.

'She's getting quite brown,' Kirsty said. 'Is she going to be a Cape Coloured?'

'That's a tan,' Dad replied. 'It's not the same.'

'Why's it not the same?' asked Calum.

'Well, that's a very good question,' said Mum, giving Dad a sharp look. 'Now go and play.'

They splashed in the sea, built sand castles and chased a ball, running back and forward to dig into the hamper, while Mum and Dad dozed in the sun.

Kirsty pointed to a low stretch of land far out to sea. 'I think that's Robben Island. I know someone there.'

'How could you know anyone there, Kirsty?' Mum murmured, half asleep, eyes hidden under her sunglasses.

'I do! The school gardener told me – it's a prison. His son's locked up there.'

Calum and Kirsty were scraping the last of the cherry trifle when they noticed some black children raking in a bin nearby.

'Can't we give them something?' asked Dad.

Mum seemed embarrassed. 'There's nothing left,' she said, tidying away the paper plates.

Dad rolled up his towel. 'Come on. Time we were going.'

When they arrived home, Martha, the De Groot's servant, was sitting on the stoep next door, a baby on her knee. An old black woman sat beside her. The family crowded round.

'Who's this wee one?' asked Mum.

'My son,' smiled Martha. Her eyes never left his face. '*Ouma* here brought him to see me. My Christmas present.'

'Is he coming to live here with you?' asked Kirsty, excited at the thought.

'No,' said Martha.

'Why not?'

Mum nudged her. 'Sshh, Kirsty!'

'He's beautiful,' said Dad quietly, holding the baby's hand.

Ouma didn't speak, just nodded, looking into the distance.

It was a Sunday morning. Dad had the record player on, and Paul Robeson's voice filled the house. Kirsty followed Calum downstairs for breakfast, and saw Dad standing very still at the open front door in a stream of sunlight, listening:

*Goin' home, goin' home,*
*I'm jes' goin home,*
*Quiet-like, some still day,*
*I'm jes' goin home.*
*It's not far, jes' close by,*
*Through an open door;*
*Work all done, care laid by,*
*Goin' to fear no more.*

Suddenly there was a scream from the back garden, and Peggy fell into the kitchen, blood trickling down her chubby legs. 'Cut!' she howled. 'Sore cut!'

Paul Robeson's voice skidded to a stop. Mr. De Groot appeared at the back door, blocking the light. 'We don't want your daughter's dirty naked bottom in our garden, thank you. I've put up a fence – barbed wire – to keep her out.'

Mum and Dad stood speechless. Calum laid down his toast. 'Don't you know my wee sister's bottom once sat on Paul Robeson's knee?'

Kirsty was amazed. What was happening? Calum never spoke like that, not to grown-ups, anyway.

'And mine too!' she joined in – she didn't want to be missed out of *that* story. But Mr. De Groot was gone. 'My bum too!' she called after him. 'My bum too!'

'Enough, Kirsty!' Mum snapped, wiping Peggy's cuts with a wet flannel.

'Yes,' agreed Dad, shutting the back door. 'We'll deal with it.'

'You should,' said Calum. 'The De Groots stink. And so does this place. Why did we ever come here?'

Kirsty could think of lots of reasons.

'Let's just get on with breakfast,' said Mum.

'I don't want my breakfast. I want to know why we came here.'

'You know why. Dad was ill. His lungs needed the sun, and –'

'Because, Calum...' Dad interrupted Mum. He was speaking quietly now, as if something was very wrong, 'because I was naïve.'

'What does naïve mean?' asked Kirsty.

'It means he was stupid,' said Calum. 'I want to go home.'

Calum was getting more and more miserable. He refused to go to school. Mum and Dad seemed tense all the time, and the word *Apartheid* kept coming up. Kirsty could hear them talking in their bedroom late at night: 'We're fiddling while Rome burns,' Dad said. But what did that mean? He played the piano, not the violin, and what had Rome got to do with it? Why was it burning? And there was a poem Dad had found – she'd seen it on his piano music stand, and heard him reading it out to Mum one day. Kirsty couldn't understand it – about a child from a place called Nyanga, who only wanted to play in the sun, but he was lying in a police station with a bullet in his head. He wasn't dead, though – he peeped through windows and became a giant travelling through the whole world. The poet had drowned herself at Three Anchor Bay near Cape Town, and was the same age as Mum. There were so many questions Kirsty wanted to ask, but she was getting scared of what the answers might be. Dad was worried about one of his students, a Cape Coloured man called Peter, who was often at the house, usually in tears. There was Joe too, a black student, who came for private piano lessons, but he hadn't been seen for ages. Dad didn't know what had happened to him, and there was talk that the police might raid the house. They'd been to the door already.

One evening Kirsty heard crying in the lounge. Calum was on the sofa, his whole body heaving, Mum and Dad on either side, hugging him.

'What's wrong?' Kirsty asked, frightened.

'Nothing,' said Dad. 'He's just happy! We all are!'

'We're going home,' sobbed Calum. 'We're going home.'

It wasn't the same, though, going home. Two years had passed, and the same ship looked different somehow, not quite like a palace any more. Peter, the tearful student, was there, sharing a cabin with Dad and Calum. He'd had to leave his wife and baby behind in Cape Town. Dad was going to try to find him a job in Scotland, and then his family would follow. Kirsty wondered if there might be a brass band to welcome him in Southampton – that would cheer him up – but Mum told her not to talk about it, she would only upset him even more.

Kirsty stood on deck as the ship sailed out of Table Bay. She couldn't bear to leave – South Africa was home now, in spite of the worries. Spring was moving into summer, and all she could think of were the things she was going to miss – her school friends, the brightness of everything, the sun, the sea, and the parties. But Mum and Dad said it was no place to bring up children. Peter was standing next to her, his bloodshot eyes looking out to Robben Island. Maybe he knew the gardener's son, but she decided not to ask.

She hadn't seen much of the gardener before she left, and she'd missed their chats. She'd been called into the Head Teacher's office.

'It's not appropriate, Kirsty. Not at Springville. I've had a word with him about it.'

After that, if they happened to see each other at break time, the old man looked away.

The ship steamed North into autumn, the weather cooler now, the Equator far behind. Kirsty had refused to go up on deck to be dunked by Neptune. She wondered how her chameleon would be getting on out in the garden. She wasn't allowed to bring it with her, and was told she'd have to give it back to her school friend. She planned to sneak it on board in her pocket, but in the muddle of removals, it had disappeared. Then, when the house was almost empty, and Mum was giving the place a final clean, she swiped it onto the floor with her cloth. 'It was shelf-coloured, Kirsty – I didn't notice it!' Mum put it out in the garden. Kirsty was certain a cat or even a snake must have eaten it by now.

Snow fell on the day she went back to her old school, and the sky was grey. The classes were mixed – girls and boys, not like Springville's – and there was no uniform. She wore new tartan trousers, and hated them. The wool was scratchy like her old kilt when she sat on Paul Robeson's knee. Everyone in the classroom kept looking at her. Not a single face was familiar, and no-one seemed to remember her either. 'The new girl', they called her.

At break time, they were each given a bottle of milk. The crate had been standing near the heating pipe that ran round the skirting board, and the smell of the luke-warm creaminess made Kirsty feel sick. She was heading towards the classroom door when, through its low window, she saw a black boy staring at her. Her heart thumped. For a moment she thought it was the child in the poem, the one from Nyanga with a bullet in his head who wasn't dead and peeped through windows. But this boy wasn't a giant – he looked small.

'That's the darkie,' said a girl standing next to her. 'He's new too.'

Out in the freezing playground, he was on his own. Kirsty wondered if he'd come on the same ship, though she hadn't seen any black children there. Maybe he was South African.

She went up to him and asked.

'No. I'm Scottish,' he said. 'Where are you from? You talk different.'

She wanted to say 'South Africa', but she wasn't sure. Did you have to be a certain colour to come from somewhere?

'I don't know,' she said.

She was homesick. She was sure of *that*. Especially today in the cold.

# The Apple Tree

AFTER THE PHONE call, they couldn't sleep. They lay in bed, husband and wife, eyes to the ceiling, fingers meshed. It was midwinter, and dawn would be late, so there was no hurry. They knew they'd be on the road in the morning, heading North, but couldn't face packing yet. Nothing to be done now, anyway. Iain's mother was gone. No warning. Her heart had stopped. She was still in bed, according to his brother, would stay there till the undertaker came. And that might be a while on Hogmanay.

Maria imagined her mother-in-law's cold limbs between the icy sheets. Wind from the Minch would be whistling up the croft, buffeting round the gable ends, rattling the windowpanes. The peat would still be glowing in the grate, the clock ticking on the mantelpiece. Her dog would know.

'Remember the picnic,' said Iain, reaching for the memory in the dark, 'when her daft dog protected those cooked chickens she'd bought? Ran like a bullet when that other mangy mutt appeared along the path. Never thought The Lump was capable of speed.'

Typical of Iain, thought Maria, to deflect from his pain with humour. He loved his mother, but could never speak of it.

'Yes,' she replied, 'that was a shining day, the picnic.'

Effie MacRae had been a widow most of her life. She was never extravagant. But she could surprise you, and splash out, as she did that day, when she slipped from Iain's car into the butcher's, and bought two whole chickens, roasted on a spit, dripping with warm, mouth-watering fat. And she always knew how to welcome you – scones and pancakes galore on arrival, crowdie from her own cow's milk, and jam, succulent with plump strawberries she'd tended and picked in her garden.

Effie's fingers weren't just green, Iain said – they were emerald, and her garden was the jewel of Braebac. That was where Maria first met her mother-in-law, on a still September afternoon, by the apple tree, the only one in the village. Effie was standing under its laden boughs, filling an old peat creel with the fruit, when Iain and Maria arrived. She gave one to Maria, who bit into its red skin, juice from the crisp, white flesh trickling down her chin. She'd never tasted such a delicious apple, sweet and subtly aromatic. She took three more from the creel, and to Effie's great delight, juggled them, right there, under the tree. And when Colm was born, Effie held her new grandson in her arms and sang *'Craobh nan Ubhal'* to him.

'It's about an apple tree,' Iain had told Maria. 'One of the oldest Gaelic songs – light years before Christ.'

Maria loved being married to a Gael, this big man, with a voice like peat. There was romance in the language, its lilt exotic compared to the flat tones of Surrey, where her own mother lived. She'd always felt rootless, an officer's only child, shipped around the colonies, and finally, when her parents separated, sent to boarding school in England. She hadn't known a feeling of community till she met Iain. Effie's island croft in the village of Braebac was an idyll in her mind; people dropped in and out of one another's houses with gifts – a bucket of fresh mackerel, or newly dug potatoes. And she never ceased to marvel at the box posted to their Edinburgh flat every month, a dozen Braebac eggs, each one swaddled in newspaper, perfectly intact.

'An idyll?' Iain mocked Maria's enthusiasm. 'It's a lethal concoction of church, gossip, and wall to wall TV soaps.' He never mentioned alcohol, the worm in the apple she tried to ignore, that she hadn't bargained for when they met. He'd been 'on the wagon' then.

He turned over in bed, away from her. 'I feel I'm disappearing,' he said, 'like one of your tricks.' His voice cracked through the dark, thinner than eggshell. 'I need a drink.'

'Can't we just lie quiet?' Maria asked, but he was already out of bed.

Two hours later, he stumbled back into the room, and flopped down beside her, snoring.

The forecast wasn't good next morning – snow from the West later in the day, so Maria got going and packed the car, anxious to get on the road. Iain dragged himself out of bed, and, fuelled with coffee, settled at the steering wheel. His eyelids drooped, and his face was as grey as the Firth of Forth.

'Are you *sure* you're up for driving, Iain?' Maria asked him.

'You mean, am I still pissed? Why don't you say what you're thinking?'

'I'm only offering – take it or leave it.'

'I've told you already, I'm fine. And anyway, it gives me something to do. I don't want to be just sitting for hours in the passenger seat, with only Mum on my mind.'

Colm whimpered in the back.

'I've got something for you, darling!' Maria called to him over her shoulder, as she reached into her bag. 'Your favourite!' She slid a cassette into the player on the dashboard.

'I can do without Postman bloody Pat right now, Maria,' groaned Iain. 'Specially in Gaelic. It's surreal.'

'I just thought... OK, we'll switch it off,' she sighed, pressing the stop button. Colm wailed in protest. She reached into the back and stroked his small hand.

'He'll be asleep soon anyway,' said Iain. 'The car always sends him off.'

Maria looked out at the heavy clouds.

'Let's not try to fall out, love.'

'I'm not falling out. I told you, I'm fine.'

Colm began to snooze at last, and Maria gently extracted her hand from his.

'I fancy an apple,' she said, digging in her bag again. 'Do you want one?'

'No thanks.'

She bit into the crisp, juicy flesh. 'Almost ten years since I met Effie. D'you remember? Under the apple tree. That's the best painting you've ever done – the way you captured the moment, the autumn light. Perfect.'

'I'll never forget her face when you told her you were a magician,' Iain laughed dryly. 'Might as well have declared you were a Catholic. Don't think she ever got over it.'

'That's not true! She liked my juggling. And my handkerchief trick was her favourite – she always asked me to do it!'

Maria watched Iain's hands on the steering wheel. Strong and earthy, yet elegant, with long fingers. An artist's hands, no doubt about it. She remembered him gutting a fish once, in Effie's kitchen sink, quick and firm, wielding the knife with breathtaking deftness. The same swift sweep she loved to watch when his paintbrush stroked a canvass – it made her dizzy, pierced the pit of her stomach.

'I failed her,' he said staring out through the windscreen. 'An artist, for God's sake, a graven image maker. And then I go and marry a magician. It's like I gave her the two fingers.'

'What do you mean!' Maria objected. 'She gave your apple tree painting pride of place in her house. She'd never have done that if she thought you were a failure.'

'A one-off. A lapse in faith on her part.'

Maria was losing patience. 'She loved you. You know she did.'

'Yes, but she'd have loved me more if I'd been a teacher, or a dentist, like Angus Morrison down the road – even a plumber, like James.'

'Don't be daft. She never loved James more than you.'

'I'm not so sure,' he replied. 'He's always been there for her – the 'good' son.'

'Maybe, but it was his choice – nobody asked him to build a house next door.'

'I'm just saying, he's been there for her, and I haven't.'

'Well, he never had to move away. When did anyone train to be an artist in Braebac?'

'I know, but she hated it. Art. Couldn't see the use in it. She has a point.'

'Had,' Maria corrected him. His negativity was getting to her.

'For fuck's sake,' he growled, 'no need to rub it in.'

'Sorry, love,' she said, resting her hand on his. 'I didn't mean – it's just when you get into this black denial of yourself, of what you do, what you are…'

'Just leave it – I'm driving!'

He was upset, and she understood, of course. But it came on her again, as it often did. A bleakness. They were so different – the attraction of opposites, she supposed. He was tall and dark, heavily built, with coiled hair that swept his shoulders like smoke. She was small and thin, her cropped blonde hair straight and spiked. A different landscape in their voices – in their minds too, she sometimes thought.

Snowflakes flecked the windscreen half way up the A9. An hour later the world was white.

'We won't make it to Braebac today,' said Iain, his focus on the road intense. 'Better stop at the first hotel that's open.'

Colm was awake, whimpering. Maria gave him some bread and juice. Then she rummaged in her bag for three tangerines, and juggled them to keep him entertained.

'Oranges in snow,' smiled Iain, 'I like that.'

He was hers again, he was with them. 'You should paint it,' said Maria.

'I might. Reminds me of home, when James and I were kids. Mum always gave us oranges at Hogmanay.'

They crawled along the road for another half hour, until a building loomed, just visible through the windscreen's sifting layers. The lettering on the sign was obliterated, but Iain drove in between the stately gateposts. The hotel seemed suspended, a ship afloat in snowfall. Festive lights looped around the eaves, and the windows throbbed with warmth. A huge snowman stood in the car park, sporting a black top hat, pipe in mouth, and an arm that curved to his hip like the handle of a jaunty teapot.

'D'you think he's the proprietor?' Iain joked, lifting Colm up to the mute face.

'Mummy's hat!' said the little boy.

'Yes, it's just like mine,' laughed Maria. 'Maybe there's a surprise inside!' and she raised the brim for Colm to have a peek.

'All gone,' he piped, 'all gone!'

'Let's hope there's room at the inn,' said Iain, as they stamped snow from their shoes on the entrance hall mat.

A friendly young woman in a tartan skirt led them upstairs. They threaded their way along a tartan-carpeted corridor, past a stuffed fox in a glass case, to a vacant family room. It was small, but comfortable, and they were soon installed. Maria played with Colm on the bed, while Iain filled the kettle and laid out cups.

'Did you ring the theatre?' he asked.

'Yes. I called first thing. They'll get the understudy in.' Miraculous Maria playing the Fairy Godmother was about as remote as Mars right now. The hotel was quiet, no sound from other rooms, the air outside hushed, as if a blanket had descended for miles around. 'It doesn't seem real,' she thought.

'It's like we're in some strange time zone,' said Iain, reading her mind. He crossed to the window and stared out at the shrouded dusk. 'No-one in the world but us.'

They ordered supper to be brought to their room.

'Shouldn't we ring James, tell him we won't be there tonight?' suggested Maria.

'You do it. I don't want to speak to him right now. And I couldn't face Ishbel if she picks up the phone.'

Maria felt Iain was a bit hard on his sister-in-law. It wasn't Ishbel's fault that she hadn't had much of an education. 'Rubbish,' he'd say. 'She was born like that. I pity anyone who tries to open a door in *her* closed mind. You'd need a crowbar.'

Ishbel's voice crooned down the line from Braebac: 'Oh, dear, that's a shame. You'll miss seeing Effie, then. The undertakers are coming this evening.'

'Couldn't they wait till tomorrow?' asked Maria.

'I don't think so, dear. We can't have the remains lying in the house for another night.'

The remains? Maria pictured a bin-bag of leftover spare ribs picked at by crows on the roadside. 'Iain really wants to see his mother one last time,' she insisted, 'and so do I.'

'Well, that may be,' nipped Ishbel, 'but it's not the way we do things here.'

'Can I have a word with James?' Maria asked, rolling her eyes in Iain's direction.

'Told you,' he mouthed from the bed, where Colm slept in his arms.

'Well, alright – if you want,' Ishbel relented, 'but I don't think he'll say any different.'

'No problem,' James slurred. 'I'll sort it out.'

Maria tidied Colm's clothes, and began to get ready for bed.

'I'm going to the bar for a dram,' said Iain.

Her heart sank. She didn't want their cocoon to be breached, this little bit of consolation from the weather god. 'You could ask room service to bring one up for you. I love it in here, just the three of us.'

But he was already on his way out. 'It's Hogmanay, for Christ's sake! I think a dram and some company might be in order.'

Maria reached for the remote, and switched on the TV. Celebrity revellers roared at a joke she'd just missed. She snapped it off. The bleakness had descended again. Suddenly she longed for her mother's voice, reserved, caring, reliable. Then she realised she hadn't told her that Effie had died. In their hurry to leave Edinburgh before the snow came, she'd forgotten to call her. She picked up the phone and dialled Surrey, but it rang out, and the voicemail clicked on: 'Please speak after the bleep.'

It didn't seem right to leave news of death on an answerphone. Maria found herself saying in a shockingly perky voice: 'Happy New Year for tomorrow, Mum – or *Bliadhna Mhath Ur*, as they say up here!'

The sky was clear in the morning, and the roads were black again. The snow ploughs had done their work. Colm waved to the snowman as they drove off.

'Happy Year!' he sang out.

'I wish you'd speak Gaelic to him,' said Maria. 'I love to hear it on the phone when you talk to your...'

'To my Mum, yes, I know. Gaelic's going the same road as her. If it's not dead, it's dying.'

'I don't see why. I mean, you could start speaking it with James. You both spoke Gaelic to Effie.'

'Yes, but never at school.'

'What – not even in the playground?'

'No. So why would we bother now?'

'For Colm. I'd like him to know it.'

'I'm telling you, it's had its day.'

'Oh, right,' said Maria, resorting to sarcasm, 'so you're saying it's inevitable?'

'As inevitable as the melting snow,' sighed Iain, weary of the subject.

'Or your love affair with alcohol.'

There was a pause as they both took in what she'd just said. Then Iain rammed his foot down on the accelerator.

'My mother may be dead, but by God, Maria, she's alive in you!'

The ferry wasn't running on New Year's Day, so Iain had called a friend who'd agreed to take them across on a small one-man ferry he operated during the summer months. They reached Braebac by mid afternoon. Once he'd switched off the ignition, Iain stayed in the driver's seat for a moment, looking at the house. Peat smoke rose from the chimney, as it always did, whatever the season. Its thick, sweet scent hung on the damp air and drifted into the car as Maria opened the passenger door. A strange noise came with it, a low moan, barely audible. She glanced at Colm, but he was asleep in the back. Then she realised. It was Iain. He was crying, but she hadn't recognised the signs, because she'd never seen him do it before. He held out his hand and she took it in hers.

'I just ca... can't,' he stammered, 'just can't... oh, God...'

Every chair in the sitting room was taken. Ishbel was bustling about, serving scones and pancakes to neighbours. James was dispensing drams. Broc, the dog, otherwise known as The Lump, moped at the hearth. The greetings were sombre and brief.

'Go on up,' James said to Iain. 'She's still in her room. Leave Colm down here with us.'

Together they climbed the stairs. Iain paused on the landing by the mahogany tallboy, and brushed a finger across the huge, dusty bible laid out on top – the only book in the house.

Maria leaned into his shoulder. 'Will we go in, love?'

'Aye,' he nodded.

The window was ajar, and the closed curtains billowed gently. Low winter light filtered through their thin folds, rippling over Effie's face. The bed appeared to be almost rocking, like a submerged boat just below the sea's translucent surface. A trick of light washed the years from the old woman's high, wide brow, erased the lines beneath her eyes, and filled out her sunken cheeks. She looked like a sleeping, grey-haired girl, hands crossed above her breasts.

'*A mhàthair, mo ghràidh,*' murmured Iain, as he knelt beside the bed, laying a hand on hers.

Maria had enough Gaelic to know he'd found the words at last to tell his mother he loved her.

The clock on the sitting room mantelpiece chimed seven, and a sleek black car purred down the track. The undertakers had arrived. Iain and James helped them carry the coffin downstairs and out into the dark. The heart had gone from the house, it seemed.

Maria began to get Colm ready for bed.

'I'll take Broc for a walk,' Iain said to her. 'Poor old Lump – he looks lost.'

By half past eight Maria was snuggled under the duvet, reading a story to Colm. Iain came upstairs and sat on the bed with them.

'It's cold out,' he said, stroking Colm's forehead. 'Lots of stars.'

The child smiled and slipped into sleep. Maria whispered, not to wake him. 'It's weird, isn't it, being in the house without her.'

'I know,' Iain nodded. 'You can feel the emptiness pressing through the walls.'

'Iain!' Ishbel's voice split the quiet air. 'Iain? That's the elders coming now! Time you were down!'

He got up from the bed. 'God, that woman. The sensitivity of a clootie dumpling.'

'Why have the elders come?' Maria asked.

'What do you think? To pray for our souls. That's what they do here – gather at the house, every night till the day of the funeral. Small chance any of us'll make it through the pearly gates, though – even Mum, no matter how hard she tried. And, by God, she tried.'

'Should I come down with you?'

'It'll be all men. You'll feel like a fish out of water.'

'What about Ishbel?'

'She'll be in the kitchen, buttering pancakes and cream crackers for them all.'

'I might make an appearance in my cloak of invisibility,' smiled Maria.

'Wouldn't work,' he twinkled in that dark way of his she loved. 'The Mullahs of Braebac have x-ray eyes.'

'What about supper?'

'Don't worry. Kate next door's just been round with soup and sandwiches, and buckets of scones.'

Then he turned at the door and grinned, 'We'll dine when the hoodie crows have gone!'

Maria switched off the light, and lay in the dark next to Colm. Gaelic psalms floated up from the sitting room below – the human voice reaching out, enfolding. Strange music, this, she thought – unaccompanied, austere, yet elaborate with its own adornment, notes twisting around themselves like golden knots. She'd never been particularly religious. Her parents had taken her to church once in a while, during holidays from boarding school – Church of England, a gentle affair, the three of them standing there, singing – that's all she could remember about it. But her mother stopped going when the marriage broke down. Nevertheless, Maria always felt vaguely attracted to the idea of religion, the opportunity of ritual, faith in the unknown. 'It's the magician in you,' Iain would tease her. 'All that hocus pocus.' She knew that Iain and Effie hadn't seen eye to eye on such matters, though she'd never really understood why. After all, she thought, there was a fierce warmth here, a deep comfort in the way these people gathered around their bereaved, and nursed them through the shadow of loss; something atavistic, necessary, solid as rock. She felt proud that this was part of her son's inheritance.

She missed pottering about the croft with Effie, and didn't feel welcomed by her in-laws, who seemed to have moved in for the time being. Effie's cow, Nancy, was old now, and dry, so there was no milking to be done, but Colm enjoyed feeding the hens. Maria took him out to the garden one morning.

'No flowers – all gone!' he said, practising his favourite phrase.

'They're just asleep,' she explained, leading him to Effie's apple tree. They stood under its bare winter branches, and Colm stroked the bark.

'Apple tree,' said Maria. 'Craobh nan ubhal. Can you say that?'

'Coo nan ool,' he cooed, enjoying the sound.

Back in the sitting room, she held him up to Iain's painting, and pointed to the tree.

'Coo nan ool,' he said again and again, 'coo nan ool!'

'You see,' Maria smiled at Iain, 'your son's learning Gaelic!'

'Thought he was talking about Nancy the Coo,' said Iain, not looking up from his book.

The elders came round for four nights. As soon as they'd gone, James switched on the TV and cracked open the whisky. The brothers sat in silence, glued to the screen, watching the snooker, eating supper and downing drams, while their wives dined in the kitchen. Maria wondered about the funeral arrangements, what to do with Colm.

'Kate's daughter next door will have him,' said Ishbel, chewing on a ham sandwich.

'Can we help in any way?' offered Maria. 'Organising things…'

'Don't worry, it's all in hand.'

'Well, we'll obviously contribute to the cost.'

Ishbel gave no response.

'Do you think I could perhaps say a few words at the service?' Maria asked. 'Something about Effie, and her garden – the apple tree?'

Ishbel almost choked on her sandwich. 'Goodness, no!' she

coughed, and took a slug of tea to clear her throat. 'The ministers will be dealing with all of that!'

Mist came in from the North on the day of the funeral. Stray snow wreaths lay tucked in folds by the hillside path that led to the church. Maria stood with Iain, three rows from the front.

'I'm damned if I'll stand in the firing line,' he'd hissed at Ishbel, when she'd tried to usher him into the front, next to her and James.

Maria had never been to this church before. Its Spartan appearance surprised her. The damp, whitewashed walls were bare, the floor covered in cracked linoleum. The congregation was a sea of black, every pew filled. There was no organ, no music to ease the atmosphere.

'Where's the coffin?' Maria asked Iain.

'Out in the lobby, by the front door.'

'Yes, but... they're bringing Effie in, aren't they?'

Iain gave a harsh wee laugh. 'This isn't about her.'

'What do you mean? Of course it is!'

'I think you'll find it isn't. Look – here they come, the hoodie crows.'

Three ministers took their places by the pulpit, perched like ravens.

'We're in for a treat,' Iain muttered, 'a stiff triple measure. We'll all be on the floor.'

His cheek muscles twitched the way they always did when he was tense. Maria slipped her hand into his as the first of the ministers stepped up. She listened, but his words didn't make sense. They were so far from what she'd expected that she couldn't immediately decode their meaning. To her utter astonishment, she realised that this gaunt stranger was haranguing her, accusing her – and everyone gathered there – of not attending church as often as they should. She suppressed an instinct to heckle, to challenge his presumption – how did *he* know when she last went to church? And if he wasn't referring to her, then why wash the parish's dirty linen in public, today, of all days? Didn't this man know that people had travelled a long way to celebrate Effie's life? He was talking of fires being kindled by Jehovah's breath, like a stream of brimstone, he said, condemning them all to hell for their sins, even for being born, it seemed. Each head was bowed in submission, a pool of unbearable shame. Hail beat on the high, arched windows, and the minister raised his voice, relishing the contest. A shiver rippled through the congregation, as if it had blurred into one creature. Then the hail subsided, and sunlight pierced the gloom – a single beam resting on the nape of Ishbel's neck. The little patch of white flesh looked so vulnerable, Maria wanted to reach out and kiss it, tell her sister-in-law to hold her head high. When would these holy men begin to talk about Effie, speak her name? When would words of comfort be offered, thanks given for her life, the woman they'd all known and loved?

The second minister was speaking now, voice like a bull. He rocked rhythmically from side to side, and the floorboards creaked. Maria heard mention of a tree, an apple tree, in a beautiful garden – Effie's garden, she thought, tears of relief welling in her eyes. Effie's apple tree, *Craobh nan Ubhal*. But, no, that wasn't it – he was talking of Eden. The sin of Eve, the apple she plucked from the tree to poison the world with knowledge. Maria looked at Iain. His face was so white his features seemed to have melted.

The day felt like a shipwreck. Somehow Iain managed to play his part, shouldered the coffin with the pallbearers up to the cemetery, and took his place at the graveside. Maria straggled behind the procession of men, the only woman among them, but she didn't care what they thought. She watched Iain as he held one of the cords and lowered his mother into the earth.

The last of the mourners had left Effie's house. Maria and Ishbel were in the sitting room, clearing up, Iain and James glued to their armchairs, opening another bottle of whisky. The atmosphere was like a loaded gun. Ishbel fired the first shot:

'I don't know what you were thinking, Maria, going to the graveside. It just isn't done. Didn't you tell her, Iain?'

'He told me, Ishbel,' said Maria, quietly intervening.

'Course I *told* her!' Iain flung the word over his shoulder. 'But she's a grown up. Her choice.'

'It's nothing to do with choice,' Ishbel insisted.

James leaned across the hearth to fill up his brother's glass. 'I'm afraid,' he mumbled, with a weak, conspiratorial smile, 'it's a case of *when in Rome...*'

'I didn't know you'd turned Catholic, James!' Ishbel chastised her husband. 'It's about respect. For how we do things here.'

'Aye, that's just it,' said James, flopping back into his seat. 'That's what I'm saying.'

'Iain needed me, Ishbel,' Maria explained. 'The service wasn't exactly comforting. It was... I mean, no mention of Effie, her life... it could have been *anyone's* funeral!'

'It's not for the deceased,' replied Ishbel, her anger rattling the teacups as she cleared them onto a tray.

'Or the living,' Iain laughed to himself. 'No siree!'

'A funeral's a warning, a warning to us all,' Ishbel continued, cleaving to her dignity.

Maria knew she should let it alone, but somehow she couldn't. 'Well, it wasn't easy to get through.'

'It's not *meant* to be easy!' Ishbel fumed.

'You're right there!' thundered Iain, rising from his chair. 'It's what it's meant to be – a crucifixion of your feelings, a slaughter of your bloody soul. Spiritual fascism, that's what it is!'

James hauled Iain back into his seat. 'Wheesht, Iain! You'll be getting yourself snookered, talking like that – snookered, just!'

'Your brother's a disgrace, James,' said Ishbel, piling sherry glasses on top of the wobbling teacups.

'It's only the drink talking,' James reassured her, 'that's all. Only the drink.'

'Will you listen to the pot calling the kettle!' she hit back.

'Why don't you two bugger off next door to your own house and leave us in peace?' growled Iain.

Maria put her hand on his shoulder: 'Iain! Please, love…'

'Come on now, let's all calm down,' said James. 'A bit of relaxation. How about one of your tricks, Maria? That one you do with the hanky, eh?'

'For goodness' sake!' spluttered Ishbel, disgusted.

James reached into his pocket. 'I've got one here somewhere.' He swayed on his feet as he dug deep, and pulled out a crumpled grey rag. 'There you go!' he said, triumphantly, presenting it to Maria. 'Can you make it disappear?'

Maria took the thing, but couldn't think what to say.

'Smashing!' laughed James, rubbing his palms in what looked like genuine anticipation. 'Let's watch the magic, then! Go on, Maria! Go on!'

'Well… I… I… alright,' she stammered, 'if you… if you're sure you really… Abradadabra…' and gave the cloth a feeble flourish.

James exploded with drunken laughter: 'Will you look at that! Did you see that? It's gone! My flipping hanky's gone!'

'What are you thinking, James!' gasped Ishbel, slamming down the tray, sherry glasses and teacups rolling onto the table, 'and your mother just buried! Give that filthy article back to him, Maria, wherever you've put the horrible thing!'

Iain had sunk forward in his chair, his head in his hands. 'This is unbelievable!' he moaned, rocking back and forward.

'Would… would anyone like a cup of tea?' ventured Maria.

'Never mind tea,' said Ishbel, thumping the crockery back onto the tray. 'There's all these sherry glasses and plates to tidy up first.'

Iain leapt to his feet again and lunged at the table. 'I'll tidy up your fucking sherry glasses for you!' he roared, sweeping the lot to the floor.

They stood for a moment in silence. Broken glass and china twinkled among cold tea puddles soaking into the carpet.

'That man of yours is totally out of control, Maria,' said Ishbel, with a terrifying calm that defied response. 'I'll clear this mess. You'd better go and pick up your child from next door. I expect they'll have had enough of him by now.'

Later that afternoon, Maria was peeling potatoes at the kitchen sink, Colm babbling at her feet. She heard the front door slam, so hard the walls shook. She went through to the sitting room. Only a few minutes ago, Iain had been stretched out on the sofa, snoozing, but he was gone. James was slumped in Effie's armchair, staring at the peat flames, and Ishbel was standing in the middle of the room, strangely still, a piece of paper in her hand.

'Is everything alright?' asked Maria.

Without a word, Ishbel handed her the paper. It was Effie's will. The simple statement made it clear that everything had been left to James.

'Would you mind watching Colm for me?' Maria asked, handing the document back to Ishbel. 'I have to see if Iain's alright.'

'Aye,' mumbled James, through a whisky haze. 'No problem.'

Iain stood alone on the brae, a silhouette in the dusk. Maria caught up with him, and they continued along the track in silence for a while. At last she spoke:

'I read it. The will. Did you know about it?'

He walked on a few paces before he replied. 'No.'

She thought she detected a tremor in the single word, but had never seen him more dignified.

'No,' he said again, 'I didn't.'

They were heading along the top road now, Effie's house below them, the croft sweeping to the shore like a brown winter blanket.

'Did I ever tell you,' said Iain, 'we don't tend to say 'I own' in Gaelic? It's not a verb we use.'

'So what *do* you say then?'

'Things are *at you*. Or *with you*. Way back, a hundred years ago, folk shared, took turns – a rolling system – runrig, it's called, where you each had a shot at the good land.'

Maria looked down at Effie's house again, its whitewashed stone a dim eye in the fading light. 'It's the garden that breaks my heart,' she said. 'The apple tree. Not being able to come here and pick apples with Colm. Why on earth…? Was it what you said – the graven images, and marrying me?'

'It didn't help, but no, it wasn't that.'

'Well, what then?'

'She was right,' said Iain, looking towards the headland as they walked on. 'From her point of view, she was right. I'm not a believer. Never could be. And I told her so. It was a good few years back – before I met you. I told her because I couldn't pretend any more. I didn't sign up, so she wrote me out.'

Maria had been married to this man for almost five years. It was only now she was beginning to understand him.

'But everything?' she persisted. 'Everything? It's so extreme.'

He gave a bleak little laugh. 'Extreme is the word for normal here.'

They packed their things next morning.

'I'll drive,' Maria told him. 'You can sleep off your hangover.'

He didn't object, merely pointed out that although he'd come to bed late, he hadn't been drinking, actually. 'There was a full moon, white as a pandrop, and I went for a walk,' he said. 'Wanted to have a look at Braebac in a new light. Nearly woke you up to get you to come with me.'

'And what did Braebac look like?' she asked.

'Not home anymore.'

He was keen to be on the road. He'd strapped Colm into the back, and planted himself in the passenger seat with his newspaper, long before Maria was ready. Inside the house, she gathered the toys from the sitting room floor. James and Ishbel sat at the kitchen table, finishing breakfast in silence. Maria picked up her bags, and took them out to the car.

'That you?' Iain asked. 'Are we off, then?'

'Yes, that's me.' She settled herself into the driver's seat, and switched on the ignition, but didn't drive off.

'What are we waiting for?' Iain yawned. 'Come on. Let's get going.'

Maria opened the door, and got out of the car, the engine still running.

'There's something I need – won't be a minute,' she said, and ran back into the house.

Ishbel was on her knees in the sitting room, raking ashes at the hearth. 'Have you forgotten something?' she asked – the first time she'd spoken to Maria since she'd handed her the will the day before.

'Yes. I have,' said Maria, taking off her shoes. 'The apple tree.' She stood on the sofa, and lifted Iain's painting from its hook on the wall.

'Don't James and I own that?' said Ishbel, a statement behind the question.

'I don't think so,' replied Maria. 'And anyway, it's our turn now.'

'Hope you won't take after your mother,' Iain winked at Colm, as they drove up the hill out of Braebac. '*Cinneach*, that's what she is!'

'Coo nan ool!' Colm cooed, pointing at the painting, perched on the back seat next to him.

'Aye, that's right,' Iain nodded, 'Craobh nan Ubhal. And your mother's a cinneach! Mind that word, Colm – cinneach!'

'That wouldn't be you speaking Gaelic to your son?' smiled Maria.

'Keenyach! Keenyach!' Colm crooned.

'That's it!' laughed Iain. 'A heathen! She's obviously never heard of the eighth commandment. Nothing but a thieving heathen!'

# Chromosomes and Chocolate

I DRAG MYSELF up the stairs, the humidity unbearable. The other mothers are already ensconced in the viewing gallery, chatting. I could have been here ten minutes ago, letting the day dissolve. Why am I always late?

'Put your shoes on! Where's your jacket? Well, get your coat, then! Pick up your swimming bag *yourself,* can't you!'

I know she can't help it, but she's always so *slow*. Which makes me speed up, add the momentum she lacks, till I hear myself whining like gran's old tin spinning top we wind up and let go on the kitchen floor.

'You haven't been to the toilet, have you! Your problem. You won't be able to go once you're in the pool!'

I haul off the layers – why on earth am I wearing so much? – breasts and armpits clammy, rivers running down my back, and park myself on the hard plastic seat. Children's voices bubble in the shimmer below me. It's one of those days. The kind that hunts me, hunts me down to a place where I'm sinking without you, under the weight of the one that isn't you. I close my eyes, try to blank the long summer holidays stretched out in front of me, every day filled with this child's needs. I don't even know if she'll ever swim. Seems more committed to pulling off other children's goggles and chucking them into the deep end. The instructor's bark stabs the thick air. There's a man at the pool side with a huge ladle.

'Someone must have been sick,' says one of the mums.

Maybe I should go back down. But she looks alright, so I stay put. She's his for the next forty-five minutes. He can have her.

If I could shape the weeks ahead into some form, a structure to hang my anxieties on – a long rail of days like coat hangers, each with a new bright gown:

'Now let's see – it'll be the emerald today, crimson tomorrow, and I won't be that beige child of woe on Wednesday. I'll blaze in sunflower yellow...'

But it's just one long grey sheet, stretching out over an endless road – seven weeks of no school feels like seven years right now. I'm her playmate as well as her mother; the invitations don't come flooding in for a child with an extra chromosome, no matter how often we have her classmates round for tea. No point in asking her father to help out, share a bit of family time, even:

'I'm so busy, love – too much work on, can't possibly get involved right now.' As if I haven't got work? I'll be up all night again, trying to squeeze strikingly unoriginal thoughts from my desiccated brain onto a blank screen, battling the weekly deadline... that is, if the editor doesn't give me the boot.

What am I doing? That's five precious minutes gone, and I've wasted them. This was supposed to be a break, an oasis, just for me. I rake around in my bag for a book. But I've left it in the car, haven't I, what with the rush. The young mum next to me catches my eye, smiles vaguely – she could be you, you could be her, well, not really, but you might have been a mother by now – twenty-one, long-limbed and lovely. My girl, my young woman. You might have come with me, or could have taken her swimming for me, big sister's treat. You'd have looked like me, I think. You had the same mouth. I hold your landscape inside me, the lapping sea-loch, the granite church against the mountains, your small headstone the size of you. I've never really talked about you to her. Perhaps I should. I could take her to see you, your grave. That would swallow up a yard or two of the long grey sheet ahead.

She's sitting out of the pool now, on the edge, not joining in, fiddling with goggles, tweaking the strap – always has to have something to twine and loop around her fingers. But her own goggles are still in her swimming bag. She won't wear them – must have taken a pair from someone else. She looks lost. Small for her age. It's hard for her, I know. She's slow, everything always takes ten times longer than it does with other children, than it would have done with you. But she knows what's going on. Not the dough-ball they probably think she is. Why can't they include her? I'd better go down and have a word with them.

'I think we can call it a day,' the man says to me – the one who was carrying the giant ladle. 'She's not in the mood.'

I call to her. 'That's it – lesson's over! Time to go.'

She slides back into the pool, a slippery wee seal. I lunge and grab her foot. 'Come on! No messing around. We've had enough of that already.'

But she wriggles and thrashes. 'I want to stay in! Leave me alone!'

Everyone's watching. My bag swings round my shoulder and slaps the pool's surface. I whip it out of the water, still clutching her ankle. I may be red as a boiling lobster, but I'm going to win this one. She has to come out now. What am I doing? I'm a loving, educated woman – I've never hit her. Not once. But right now I could hold her under, I really could – almost. Her small face cracks, blue eyes sudden waterfalls. Out she comes, and I march her to the changing cubicle.

'How many times do I have to tell you? Try hard, follow instructions, and then everyone will be happy. What *is* the problem?'

I'm ripping off her swimming costume. It's flecked on the inside, with strange soft grains – brown and mustard coloured flakes all over her back.

'What on earth is this?' I ask, nonplussed.

'You said I had to wait,' she wails. 'I tried, but I couldn't.'

Things are looking up. All I had to do was make a decision – ring around, find a hotel. Must be mad! Chose the most expensive one – pure bravado, but dammit, I feel I deserve it. I've filled up with petrol, and we're on the road, heading North-West, coming to see you. Me and your wee sister, our bags in the back. The CD's blaring – *Disney* favourites, those songs that usually drill my brain till it's numb, but today I sing along with her passionate monotone.

It's early evening when we get there, an old-world grandeur to the place. Cool green drapes sweep from high windows to floor.

'A princess bed!' she whoops, clutching her little pink suitcase. 'Let's dress for dinner!'

'Where did you get that idea?' I ask.

'Beauty and the Beast,' she says.

I watch as she unzips her case, takes out the dress, necklace and best shoes she chose to pack.

I look out over the loch to the opposite shore where you lie.

'What's the matter, Mummy?'

She's a litmus paper. And I tell her about you. That we had you, for ten days. That you would have been her big sister, but you went to sleep, and didn't wake up.

'Why?' she asks.

'We don't know,' I reply. 'It's a mystery.'

'I wake up every morning,' she says.

'You sure do, and every night.'

'I'm good at waking up. Not like my big sister.'

Next day, and the sun's high as we drive over the bridge. We're coming to you. Just a picnic to buy, and then we'll wind our way down the loch. The sky's as blue as your eyes were. Sunlight slants over Ben Cruachan, the shoreline a long, wide smile.

'Not a single cloud up there,' I say, pressing the button to open the widow on her side. 'So blue.'

'Like my eyes,' she says, as if she'd invented the colour.

The shop's busy, holiday folk, relaxed in shorts and tee-shirts. I've primed her, as usual: 'Now, just stand next to me, no grabbing things from shelves.'

But she's off, flitting about between the aisles, fists full of chocolate, crisps, biscuits, eyes demonic with temptation.

'Put those back,' I hiss. I can hear myself. I've turned into a snake. 'What did I sssssay! You're sssspoiling a sssspecial day. You jusssst can't resisssst, it, can you! Ssssstop it!'

Everyone's looking. I chuck the stuff back onto the shelves, not in any order, and grab her wrist.

'I want a treat,' she whimpers.

'OK, one treat – *one*, mind,' I spit. And she selects the biggest chocolate bar I've ever seen.

'Well, you did say *one*,' chuckles a voice behind me. An elderly man is ruffling her hair. 'You're a smart cookie, aren't you, darling.'

It's amazing how a vote of confidence in her from someone else restores my faith instantly. I want to hug this stranger for getting me back on track.

'He's a kind man,' she says, giving him a wave as we drive off.

I grip the steering wheel, and tell myself: 'I should be more kind. I'll try. I will. I'll try.'

She savours her rationed treat, silence between us for a few minutes. Then she pipes up: 'Is she sleeping?'

'Who?'

'My big sister. Is she asleep?'

'Well, in a way. A long sleep. She won't ever wake up.'

'Why?'

'Because she's dead.'

'I want to see her.'

'We can't, love. When she died, we wrapped her up, and put her in a little box, far down under the ground.'

'Let's dig her up and wake her. I want to give her some chocolate.'

'We can't. She melted into the earth long ago.'

'Was she made of chocolate?'

'No, of course not.'

'Don't laugh,' she chastises me, every chromosome, especially the extra one, laden with solemnity. 'I miss my big sister.'

We draw up at the cemetery car park.

'I'm going to plant the flower we bought,' I say, 'And you can find some stones on the shore to put on her grave, if you like.'

I watch her step gingerly among rocks and sea-wrack. Uneven ground is always a challenge for her, and I hold out my hand to give support. She picks up a stone, a long grey thing, with a strange raised mark in its centre.

'I want to give her this,' she says.

'What about that one, over there' I suggest, pointing to a perfect quartz oval.

'No,' she insists. 'This is my lovely one. I like the spot in the middle.'

The small church nestles on green mossy slopes, holding its ground with quiet confidence, granite face to the South. The iron gate clangs and scrapes as we enter, and she's off again, hide and seek among the grave stones. I walk up the path to that one patch of grass imprinted on my DNA. A simple granite rectangle, quarried from rock below Ben Cruachan, lies horizontally above your head. Near to it, another headstone tells me: *'The Mountains Bring Peace To The People.'* And they do, these bens, as I kneel in their lee, planting a white rose of June, the Jacobite rose, white as the snowdrops that bloomed in the month you came, and left.

'Here's my stone,' she says, running to me, breathless. 'Where is she? Can I give it to her?'

'She's under the grass here,' I reply, patting the earth around the plant's base.

'What's her name?' she asks.

'It's there – on her stone. Read it to me.'

She screws up her face.

'Don't you like it?'

'I want to call her *Belle.* Like Beauty and the Beast. What's her stone for?'

'That's how we remember people. Stones are for remembering.'

'Like the cairn,' she says.

'Which cairn?'

'The cairn Dad made for Gran,' she reminds me, with no judgement. She doesn't detect the irony of my forgetfulness. 'I need my felt pens,' she says, 'I want to write *Belle* on mine.'

'It'll wash off in the rain. Use a piece of gravel. Stone can write on stone.'

She tries, but gives up, as always, when she fails first time. I take her hand and guide her fingers.

'Not on the spot in the middle,' she says. 'Don't cover up the special bit.'

She looks at the faint letters with satisfaction, placing her stone next to yours. 'Will Belle get married?' she asks.

'No, I don't think so.' I find myself whispering. 'She's dead.' Daft, I know, but I sense the admission might offend you.

'But *I* will,' she says, with absolute certainty. 'I'm alive.'

We drive further down the loch, and choose a picnic spot on the shore, near the place where we lived for a while, your father and I, after we married. It's over twenty years since we left the little square of council houses, built for quarry workers, decades back. There's probably no-one there that would remember me any more, but I don't want to meet anyone just now. I want to sit in the sun with thoughts of you.

Far across the glittering loch wind turbines rotate on the skyline. I sip rosé wine from a plastic glass – my treat, one of those small bottles you get on aeroplanes. She's quietly enjoying her lunch, perched on a flat-topped boulder, like the statue of Hans Andersen's Little Mermaid. It's eight years since I saw her on the hospital screen, afloat in her own universe. I knew then I didn't want any tests. I made my choice. She seems to sense my mood, and gives me that smile of hers, unfiltered, straight from the heart. We sit for a long time, no hurry, no place we have to be.

'It's a perfect day,' I sigh. 'Perfect.'

'What's perfect?' she asks. Her grace and femininity pierce me. She has the same mouth as you, and me. 'I don't know,' I say. 'I'm not sure – it's just a word.'

'It means chocolate,' she says, and for some reason, I weep with laughter.

I tell her about how I'd walk down the road between bare birch trees on frosty nights, you growing inside me, stars like shards of glass above us. How we brought you back here in your small white box, and kept you with us at home for one last night before we buried you.

'And now you've got *me*,' she says.

'I have,' I reply, drawing her onto my knee. Her warm, soft

skin smells of chocolate.

'Are you happy?' she asks.

'Yes, I'm happy.' I drain the last of my wine. 'Come on. I'll take you along the road by the birch trees.'

We walk hand in hand, the flutter of lush green leaves at our shoulders, past the houses, down to the jetty.

'I want to swim,' she says.

'What – in the loch?' and she's taking off her sandals. 'Careful,' I warn, as she starts to wade out.

'It's cold!' she squeals, then turns back, arms out for me to catch her as she slithers on seaweed. I scoop her up.

'It's not safe. You can't swim yet.'

'I know,' she shivers. 'But I will.'

# A Day Off

FOR THE FIRST time in his life, Donald had become punctual. In fact, he was early for work. Every day. He couldn't wait to see Anna. The stink of the sheds didn't matter – he'd have rolled about in the chicken muck if he'd had to, just to be with her. He liked defending her against the onslaught of Sheila's hostility. Totally unwarranted, that woman's constant carping. What was her problem? You couldn't find a more reliable worker than Anna – she put in the hours, scrupulous about every detail of the job. And she was smart. She could have run rings round Sheila if she'd wanted to, though she never did. And Sheila knew it. Maybe that was her problem.

Or maybe it was Anna's looks she couldn't take. Not that Anna was glamorous – she never wore make-up. There was nothing fake about her. She looked as if she'd walked out of the woods, Donald thought. Her brown hair fell simply to her shoulders from a centre parting, when it wasn't tied up in one of those chicken workers' protective hats. She even looked gorgeous in that – he loved the way stray wisps slipped out from under the elastic rim, brushing her slender neck. And those smoky green eyes, set above wide, high cheek bones, held a world he longed to be part of. He felt he was stepping onto its threshold, now and again, during lunch breaks, or sometimes between shifts, when she taught him a few words of Polish. Sheila couldn't stand that – it really got to her, especially when

Anna was showing the ropes to the new boy, Andreas.

'Cut that oot, will ye? We're no huvin yon gobbledygook aroon here. Ye'll stick tae English, while ah'm in charge!'

'That'll be the Queen's English, eh, Sheila?' Donald couldn't resist having a go.

'Shut it, you, and get oan wi yer work.'

It was the end of lunch break, and they were all seated round the table in the workers' shed. Donald got up and switched the kettle on again for another cuppa. He knew what was coming, so he pre-empted her: 'We've still got five minutes left, Sheila.'

'No by ma watch, ye huvnae.' She was making the most of the boss's absence, ruling the roost while he was away on holiday. 'The university's no teachin ye much if ye cannae tell the time.'

That got her goat too. She seemed to resent anyone who had a life beyond the chicken farm.

'Well, I'm certainly learning the harsh reality of economics here, Sheila. Nothing like testing theory with practice!' He wasn't letting her get away with those cheap jibes she always dished up, trying to make out he was born with a silver spoon in his mouth. He was the first in his family to go to university, and proud of it. 'Another cuppa, Andreas?'

The lad shook his head, signalling 'No.' The newest recruit, he was watching his back, particularly when Sheila was around.

'Red mites are bad in Shed Number 2, Anna,' she went on, ignoring Donald as he sat down again with two steaming mugs, one for himself and one for Anna. 'Really bad. Ye'll huv tae spray it good and thorough, mind. And check fur dead chickens in there while ye're at it.'

'I did this morning. I always do,' said Anna quietly, sipping her coffee.

'Aye, but they're no lookin good.' Sheila picked up her bag. 'Right, that's me – got tae go.'

'Clocking off early, are we?' Donald lobbed the question over his newspaper, without looking up. Ever since Hendry had gone on holiday, Sheila had been cutting her hours and upping theirs.

'Nane ae yer business,' she mumbled, lighting up a fag.

He watched from the window as she headed down the path to her battered old car. 'Does that mean you're working late again, Anna?' he asked.

'Yes,' she sighed.

Andreas said nothing, and trudged off towards Shed Number 1. The lad was still a teenager, and Donald could read homesickness all over his drooping shoulders. It was a perfect summer afternoon, grass and trees lush and luminous. Stuck inside a stinking shed with thousands of squawking birds deadening your senses was the last place you'd want to be. Tomorrow was Donald's day off. He hoped the weather would hold. Anna was due to finish at four, and they'd planned a walk in the woods nearby.

A ridge of high pressure had settled for the week. He made a picnic, and cycled along the road under a canopy of trees. The three-mile stretch from his parents' home to the farm was a tunnel of lime green light, and Anna would be at the end of it, showered and smelling of geranium soap.

But when he arrived, she was still hard at work in the scratch shed.

'Anna!' he called to her, through the din of fretting chickens. 'You were supposed to have finished an hour ago! Why are you still here?' But he knew the answer before she gave it.

'Sheila went home early. Again.'

'She's chancing it while Hendry's away. It's like she's suddenly got all this power, but not a clue how to use it. You should have phoned me. I'd have come.'

'I forget to charge mobile – battery is flat. Like me.' She looked tired. 'I forget daylight here, in chicken czysciec.'

'Czysciec?'

'Purgatory,' she translated, clearing another pile of rancid shit.

'Now there's a useful word! I'll add that to my vocab list.'

'Subject of next lesson,' she announced, spreading the clean shavings.

He loved her deadpan humour. 'Are you nearly done?'

'Yes, but I stink like hell. I have to take shower.'

Although she stayed on site in the workers' accommodation, and could get herself cleaned up quickly, Donald didn't want to miss a moment of their time together. 'You don't need to shower here. Just grab your clean clothes and a towel. We'll walk through the glen, and picnic by the pool. You can wash yourself under the waterfall – better than a power shower any day!'

And it was. She stood on a stone ledge in a long t-shirt, and laughed under the glittering torrent. He stripped to his boxer shorts and stood next to her, whooping. The water was clear and cold, straight from the hills, splashing over boulders into the deep, peaty pool below.

'Let's go for a swim!' he called, diving from the ledge. She followed him, and their squeals of laughter rang through the still woods. They sat on a huge slab of sunlit rock afterwards, and towelled themselves dry.

'Whoo! Fantastic!' Donald enthused. 'Nothing like an *al fresco* dip!'

'If we don't have Scottish rain, this would be my place for clean-up every day!' said Anna, wriggling into a fresh summer shift under her towel.

'Feel the heat of this stone,' said Donald, laying his palm on its smooth, flat surface.

'Perfect *chaise longue!*' smiled Anna, and stretched out like a cat.

This was a haunt he knew from childhood, and he'd dreamed of sharing it with her. Buzzing bees lulled the air, and blue damselflies glinted above the pool.

'My grandmother, when I am little, she always take me to river in forest like this.'

'Was that in the south of Poland?' he asked. He'd heard her mention Silesia, and had been looking at the map.

'Yes. We have many miles of beautiful pine trees.'

He took out two plastic cups from his picnic bag, and unscrewed the bottle of wine. 'How about a wee splash of vino?'

'Just small – I'm on early shift again tomorrow.'

As she took the cup, a ladybird landed on her wrist and rested there, like a polished gem.

'That's good luck,' whispered Donald, not wanting to disturb it. 'Don't know why, but definitely good luck.'

'They are health for crops,' said Anna. 'They eat thousands of aphids in their small lives. I learn about this at college.'

'But why are they called *lady*birds?'

'Because the farmers pray to our Lady to protect their harvest, and she sends them to do the good work!'

'My Gran used to have a rhyme about them,' said Donald. '*Ladybird, Ladybird, fly away home, your house is on fire and your children are gone!*'

'I never heard this,' Anna replied, 'but their black spots we call the Seven Sorrows of Mary. Strange, when their nature is for making good.'

The creature's wings opened, and it flew off over the pool.

'This is the life, eh?' breathed Donald. He felt he was expelling a whole year's build-up of Glasgow smog and hunched up studying, not to mention the relentless hours of his holiday job on the farm. 'You can take out the sandwiches, if you like, Anna. Chicken, I'm afraid. Sorry!'

She unwrapped the white slabs of pan loaf. 'My life is chicken. I am turning into chicken!'

'I've got Jaffa Cakes for afters, though,' he grinned, as if playing an ace.

'You are *connoisseur* for student food, Donald!' she teased. 'I need to give you lessons for cooking, not just my language. And show you good places to eat. We have wonderful restaurants in Wrocław, and my favourite chocolate café – best in the world!'

So – she was thinking of taking him to Poland! He raised his cup to hers with a plastic 'plunk'. 'I'm up for that! *Na zdrowie!*' he toasted.

'Cheers! Your Polish accent is good!'

'Well, you see, I've got this really brilliant teacher... this wench fae Vrozwav I'm winchin!'

'Winchin?'

'Scots for courting – you know – dating, going out?'

'Ah. Randki.'

'Rrrrrandki!' Donald rolled his 'r' for her, like a stage Scotsman, then hoped he hadn't gone too far.

But Anna was rubbing her eyes. 'Ooo. They sting. Do they look sore?'

'Yes. They do, a bit. Now you mention it.'

'I think I have allergy to red mite spray. And my feet ache like hell from those stupid regulation shoes. I am wreck!'

'You should say something to Sheila – the crazy hours she's making you work.'

'No, no,' said Anna. 'I don't want trouble. I need money to pay for my studies.'

'I know, but it drives me mad the way you're so polite.'

'It's easy for you, Donald.'

Easy? What did she mean? He was drowning in debt with his student loan, and hating the work on the chicken farm as much as she did. 'Easy?!' he protested. 'This is the worst summer job I've ever had!' As soon as he'd said it, he knew it wasn't true. 'I didn't mean... actually, it's the best job ever, Anna – meeting you...'

She took his hand with a warm formality. 'You are kind person. Thank you, Donald.'

He wanted to kiss her, but wasn't sure how she might react, so just held onto her hand.

'I have nightmares about work here. I hope it's not killing my dream.'

'Of what?' he asked.

'To become vet. Some days I forget chickens are living creatures.'

Suddenly, and in silence, a grey bird with a huge wing span rose up from the river, only yards from where they sat. Anna let go of his hand.

'What do you call it?' she asked.

'A heron.'

'Heron. This is *czapla* in Polish.'

'*Czapla*,' he repeated. '*Czapla*.'

'And you have eagles here too?

'We certainly do.'

'We say *orzel* for eagle. Our national bird – long wings like *czapla*. In Wrocław, on our town hall, we have symbol: eagle and lion – how you say, coat of wings...?'

'Of arms,' said Donald, gently correcting her, 'but I like your coat of wings better!'

They laughed and he poured more wine. 'Our flag has a lion.'

'Ah. *Lew*, we say.'

'So it's orzel and lew,' he said, placing the words side-by-side in his mind. 'The eagle and the lion – Poland and Scotland. That's you and me in your coat of wings, Anna.'

He put an arm round her shoulder. She didn't reject him. But he still wasn't sure if she wanted to be kissed. No hurry, he told himself. We've got all summer. They sat close, eating jaffa cakes. His mum always packed them for picnics when he was wee; and now, the biscuity chocolate and orange jelly blending curiously but not unpleasantly with the wine, seemed to represent something new – the flavour of this moment he'd always remember.

That was when she told him about how she might have had family here, if things had been different. Her great uncle Marek had come to Scotland during the Second World War. Her grandmother's big brother. He and a group of Polish men had somehow escaped from being slaughtered by the Russians. They reached Britain, and were put to work on the East coast of Scotland, living in tents there, all year round, building British defences. Donald imagined the stinging wind from the North Sea whistling under the canvas flaps.

'Did he go back to Poland, then, your uncle?'

'No. He died here. Pneumonia. It was a very bad winter, deep snow. The other men who lived, they stayed.'

'You could stay, Anna.' The words were out of his mouth before the thought. She disengaged herself from him, and stood up.

'I go home for study,' she said with certainty, gazing out across the river, her back to him. She looked as if she belonged here, he thought, her bare feet firmly placed on the rock, framed by old Caledonian pines. He got up and stood next to her. 'You could come back.'

'This last week, every night, I pack my case, ready to leave.'

'What? Why?' asked Donald in disbelief, his hopes suddenly evaporating.

'Chicken czysciec. And Sheila.' Then she turned, her green eyes smiling: 'Thank you for this lovely time today, Donald.'

'We should do it again. More of this, and you'll forget about packing your case.'

'If I have day off, maybe. But I have to earn money...'

'I know – rare as hen's teeth, a day off for you.'

She doubled up laughing at that. 'You say this? Hen's teeth?!'

He'd never really thought about the phrase before, but could see the funny side.

'I would like to give those poor chickens some hen's teeth!' she said. 'A day off. Open the doors, let them run out in the sunshine.' She was rubbing her eyes again. The rash around them was spreading over her forehead.

'You need to go to the doctor about that, Anna.'

She started to tidy up the picnic. 'Yes, and take time off. Sheila won't like it. She leaves all the hard shifts for me, early and late. And worst, shitty jobs.'

'I know,' he said, pouring the last of the wine.

'She doesn't resent you, like she does me, Donald. And she'll do same with this new boy, Andreas. Because he is Polish.'

She was right, he thought. Sheila was spoiling things for everyone.

'We are needed, but not wanted, me and Andreas. I think they would put us in tents if they could.'

A couple of mornings later, Anna arrived for work just as coffee break was ending. Donald could see from the set of Sheila's jaw she was spoiling for a fight. 'Mornin, Anna,' she said, drawing on her fag and then exhaling a huge cloud of smoke. 'Glad tae see ye could make it in.'

'Didn't you get my message, Sheila?' asked Anna, surprised.

'Aye. I did. So what's up wi ye?'

'I told you. I have to go to see doctor.'

'So, like, I've got tae double ma work load, wi no warnin?'

'I did double load yesterday, and day before, when you leave early. *You* gave *me* no warning, Sheila.' Anna wasn't holding back, the way she usually did. Donald hadn't seen this side of her, and liked it. He put the kettle on again. This was getting interesting.

'Aye, but I'm in charge here, when the boss is away.'

He couldn't resist chipping in. 'You know fine well you're not doing double, Sheila. I came in early to cover for Anna. You know it, and Anna knows it, 'cause we agreed it, so what's your problem?'

'Leave it, Donald. Please,' Anna insisted. 'It doesn't matter. I'm here now. I work.'

Andreas got up from his seat in the corner. 'I excuse,' he said quietly, and left to get on with his shift, head down, as he passed Sheila.

'She's got a rash from the red mite spray,' Donald went on, splashing milk into his mug, then furiously stirring it into the coffee. 'The crap goggles Hendry provides are useless.'

'We're changing over tae powder the day, anyway,' said Sheila, stubbing out her fag-end on the bare floorboards with her heel, as if she was killing it.

'Don't tell me!' he groaned. ''Cause it's cheaper?!'

'Never you mind. Nothin tae dae wi you.'

Donald looked at Anna. He couldn't bear to see her lovely jade-green eyes all red-rimmed. 'Did you get something for the rash?' he asked her.

'Yes, the doctor gave me some cream,' she said, going over to her locker.

'Well, that's something, at least,' he said, and sat down ostentatiously, unfolding his newspaper. He was going to have every minute of his coffee break – longer, maybe, and be damned.

'Aye, at my expense!' muttered Sheila, lighting up again.

'What are you on about?' Donald knew what she meant, but wasn't letting it pass.

'Swannin aff tae the doctor, at ma expense, that's whit I'm on aboot!'

'Yes,' replied Donald, slapping his newspaper down on the table, looking Sheila right in the eye, 'and when you've smoked yourself stupid, and your lungs collapse, you'll be on life support at *my* expense. D'you mind taking yourself and your fag outside?'

'Drink yer coffee and shut yer face.'

Anna was standing with her back to them at the locker door, shaking. Suddenly she swung round. Her eyes, usually cool and slightly remote, were flashing now, the rash giving them the impression of fire. 'Why do you always hit at me, Sheila? You complain you're short staffed. Hendry, he needs workers. We Polish, we do the shit work that you won't do! I need job. I work hard. I pay my taxes. I buy food in your shops.'

Donald almost cheered. He got up and took another mug off the shelf. 'You tell her, Anna!'

'Yes, I tell you! I never take benefits.'

'Aye, well, they're no for the likes o you onyroad,' said Sheila, teeth gritted.

'Did you know?' Donald was going to lay it on the line for her now, 'did you know there's more Brits claiming benefits in Germany and Spain, than Spaniards and Germans doing the same here? Like, *thousands* of our lot? Thousands. Did you know that, Sheila?'

'Dinnae gie me yer stupit university crap.'

'Coffee, Anna?' he offered jauntily.

'What *is* this? Party time?' Sheila was rattled now.

'No thanks. I work,' said Anna leaving quietly, the fire inside her suddenly extinguished.

Sheila, watched her go. 'You're wastin yer time wi that one, son. She'll make her money and bugger off back tae Poland.'

'Aye – thanks to you.' Donald sat down at the table again. He took out his mobile and texted Anna: *You were great! Don't let Sheila get you down.* Then he went back to his newspaper.

'And you can put that away! Ye're no sittin on yer erse readin rubbish on *ma* watch.'

'Five more minutes is what I'm due.'

'Ye're due nuthin, pal – *nuthin!*' Her voice was low, intense, and to his amazement, he noticed she had tears in her eyes. She spun away from him then, and faced the window. He knew he'd caught a glimpse of something she couldn't bear anyone to see. She stood absolutely still, and looked shockingly fragile, as if she might shatter into fragments if he so much as breathed in her direction. This place is making that woman ill, Donald thought. All of us. And he remembered the sickness he'd felt two weeks ago, after he'd signed that document. Hendry had told him to put his signature at the foot of the page, giving a false date for the eggs. He knew it was wrong, illegal, probably – the eggs were days older than the date stamped on them, and he shouldn't have signed. But Hendry had insisted this was 'part of his responsibilities' as an employee, and if he didn't want to do it he could walk out – they'd get someone else, no problem. Donald needed the money. And he was just getting to know Anna. He didn't want to lose the job. He turned another page of his newspaper. A face looked straight at him from a photo: an exhausted, desperate man, dragging himself and a frightened child along a beach in Greece. 'God – look at that,' he sighed.

Sheila glanced over her shoulder to see what he was referring to. Donald pointed to the photo. 'That's where Hendry is right now, living it up in his posh house. Sunny Kos, where folk are wading out the sea with only a bin bag instead of a flight case.'

'It's no Hendry's fault they're daft enough tae pay for a trip in a boat like a sieve,' she scoffed, and turned back to the window.

'Aye, well, mind when you cast your precious vote, Sheila –'

'Europe?' and she gave a strange wee laugh. 'Fuckin midden! Oh, we'll be comin oot, make no mistake.'

'It'll be that, alright,' said Donald, 'if we do.'

Sheila rounded on him, every muscle quivering. 'Listen tae yersel! Whit do you ken aboot mistakes at your age? When ye grow up ye'll see whit the *real* world's like. Ma son cannae get a job!'

'He could get one here.'

'He wouldnae touch this crap! Same as you – the minute yon lassie packs her bags for hame, you'll be oot o here an aa. Ye're only stickin in cause o her.'

Donald calmly sipped the last of his coffee. 'You know nothing about me, Sheila.'

'And you ken hee-haw aboot <u>me</u>!' She was raging now. 'Fags are the only treat I get. I've a husband at hame, sick as a dug in a wheelchair, wi his benefits cut tae the bone. I'm no skivin aff early for nuthin. I've got shite tae wipe up, day and night. You dinnae ken ye were born!' She lunged at him, and grabbed the newspaper. 'Noo, gie me yon trash ye're readin, get aff yer erse, and dae some work!'

But Donald's attention wasn't on his paper. He was standing up, looking through the open doorway. 'What the hell's going on out there?' An avalanche of squawking chickens, thousands of them, were flooding down the field from the sheds.

'Oh, my God!' Sheila gasped. 'They've been let loose! Hendry'll go daft!'

Donald's mobile jingled on the table. He picked it up and

read the text. 'It's from Anna. She's let the chickens out for some sunshine, she says. She's giving them a day off!'

'Whit?!' squawked Sheila. '*Whit*? In the name of... well, dinnae just stand there starin at yer fuckin phone! This is nae time fur textin! Get thae chickens back inside! Andreas! Andreas! Where's yon stupit wee Polish prick? *Andreas*!'

And Donald just knew. Before he'd read her next message confirming it, he knew. He ran to the farm's main gate. There she was, down the road. And that was it – his last sight of Anna, stepping with her suitcase onto the bus.

# Merryland Street

HOGMANAY, AND HE found himself back in Glasgow. He'd arrived earlier than expected – unusual for him; but family responsibilities had loosened their grip now that he was divorced and living alone. He could feel the familiar, bone-aching damp even before he'd got out of his car. Darkness and drizzle. Not the city snow-scape imagined in the play he was going to see – a version of Dickens' *Christmas Carol*, in a 'site-specific' venue. The two tickets he'd been given were a seasonal gift from a friend who was part of the production team. A kind thought, even if it felt like pity. The only person he could think to invite had just texted him to call off. They'd planned to go for a pre-show bite, but now he faced a two-hour gulf all on his own.

A police van cruised round the block as he drew in to park. A flurry to his right distracted him, and his wheel trim scraped the pavement. Four or five youths swooped by his windscreen like bats from the shadows, a movement so sudden he ducked behind the steering wheel; but just as fast, they swept round the passenger window, and were gone. He left the engine running with the fan on to combat the condensation, having struggled to clear it all the way from home in the Borders. Then he leaned over and wiped the passenger seat window. His heart lurched as he read the sign pinned to a lamp post: Merryland Street. His birthplace. He hadn't thought about it for as long as he could remember. It seemed to be just a gap site now. Maybe that's where the building had been – the nursing home, run by the Sisters of Mercy, where his mother pushed him from darkness into light.

He got out of the car and took a dander round the walls of the old town hall, illuminated for the Festive Season, he supposed, with lurid beams of purple and blue. His architect's eye traced the carving on an elaborate frieze – children pulling a chariot, eerily haloed by lamplit drizzle. Above them, words proclaimed: *Music and Drama*. And then, round the corner, over the main entrance, he picked out the shape of a handsome ship, flanked by two shipyard workers, and the Latin motto *Nihil Sine Labore*. He murmured the translation, like a mantra in the dark: *Nothing Without Work*... OK, he thought, challenging the idea – he wasn't an actual builder, but there would be none of these porticos, turrets, and falderals, if it wasn't for folk like him who designed them. He'd worked hard all his life, hadn't he? Bloody hard. Just a pity he'd picked a profession that was in free-fall, the building industry collapsing all around him. His whole life felt like rubble.

Something jabbed his back. A quick breath on his neck.

'Walk tae yer car, and keep close,' hissed a voice in his ear. 'Don't say nuthin.' A young man gripped an arm round his waist. He felt cold steel against his flesh, its edge flirting with his trouser belt. He didn't protest, though his heart was pumping. A police siren wailed a street or two away.

'I'm yer son, if they ask. Got that?'

'Got that. My son.' He'd always wanted a son, but it hadn't happened. Three daughters.

'And whit's ma name, then? Eh?'

He pressed his key and the door locks clunked their release. A police van blared round the block, lights strobing, and screeched to a halt next to his car, spraying his trousers with rain water as he climbed into the driver's seat. The young man was already sitting next to him, seat-belted and grinning.

'Shut the door, Dad! It's soakin!'

The policeman tapped on the driver's window, and signalled to wind it down. 'Your name?'

Why did he instantly feel guilty being questioned by a policeman? He couldn't think for a moment. 'My name?' The flashing blue light sliced his thoughts. 'Martin. Martin MacLeod.'

'And him?'

'This is... eh... my son. Brendan. Brendan MacLeod.' Why on earth had he said that? He opened his mouth again to retract it, but nothing came out.

'Your son, is it?' the policeman repeated.

Brendan smiled.

'Can I see yer licence?'

'Sure,' said Martin, fumbling in the glove compartment above Brendan's knees, which gaped through his slashed jeans like butchers' knuckle bones. 'Here you are.'

'And what are you doing here on Hogmanay, Mr. MacLeod?'

'I'm – we're – going to see a play in the town hall there.'

'Aye,' chirped Brendan. 'We're goin tae the theeyAYter!'

'Bit early aren't you? Doesn't start for another couple of hours.'

'We're eatin oot furst,' explained Brendan. 'Chinese, eh, Dad?'

'Uh... yes... that's right. Chinese,' agreed Martin.

'Aye, well, mind and lock up yer car,' advised the policeman. 'We're havin a bit of bother round here the night.'

'Why the hell didn't I tell him this nutter has a knife, that I'm being held hostage?' thought Martin, as the police car glided off round the corner. 'I'm a wimp. That's why my life's fallen apart. A useless wimp.'

''Mon, then! Whit are we waitin fur? Drive tae the Dragon Inn, Dad. Turn roon, then next left, left again, and keep goin.'

Brendan whipped the blade into Martin's open jacket, and poked it under his armpit. 'I'm up fur spare ribs. And a chicken Chow Mein. And deep fried ice cream fur efters. DefinEtely.'

'Look – I'll buy you a meal, I will, I promise. But please, can you put that thing away, at least while I'm driving?'

'Mibbe. If you call me Brendan. Go on. Say it. Say it, Dad.'

The knife was nuzzling each rib down his left side.

'Brendan.'

'Again.'

'Brendan.'

'At least ye didnae gie me some fuckin blue-nose name, eh? William, or cunting George! Ye'd huv been mince bi noo if ye hud!'

Martin couldn't quite work him out, this red-haired maniac, with sunken, deep green eyes, his face like an ancient child. What did he want? Was it just a meal? Company? Or was he actually going to kill him with that knife? As they passed Ibrox, Brendan suddenly brandished the weapon in the direction of the stadium, and bawled out 'Fucking WANKERS!' Martin almost lost his grip on the steering wheel, the car lurching to the left. His nerves were completely frayed.

'Steady on, Dad! Nearly hud us climbing the pavement there!'

Martin drew up at the Dragon Inn. Every building around it was boarded up. The only light in any window came from the drab little Chinese emporium, which stood waiting for them like a last outpost.

'Right,' said Brendan. 'Let's get the grub.'

'You nip in and I'll wait,' Martin suggested in a casual tone, reaching into his pocket. 'Here's a tenner.'

'D'ye think Ah'm a mug?' Brendan had read his thoughts. 'Naw, naw, pal. Ye're no gonnae drive aff. Ye're comin wi me. Get oot the motor.'

A quiet Chinese woman appeared in the dim light behind a metal grille. Brendan held Martin's arm tight, and placed his order, without even reading the menu. 'Six chicken Chow Mein, ten egg fried rice, nine sweet and sour pork, fifteen deep fried ice creams, and twenty cans of Irn Bru.'

'What?!' exclaimed Martin. 'We'll never get through that much!'

'Whit's up, Dad? Ye're no forgettin ma wee bro? Some appetite, Jamsie – an aa oor pals?'

'Party?' smiled the woman benignly.

'Aye,' grinned Brendan, moving to stand against the door. 'That's right. Hogmanay – time tae celebrate!'

'Excuse me,' Martin whispered intensely, as the woman was about to return to the kitchen. 'Could you call the police?' He was kicking himself for leaving his phone in the car.

'Peas?' she asked. 'A portion of peas?'

'Naw – we're fine,' Brendan called over to her. 'No need tae overdae it,' and she vanished behind the kitchen door.

They stood waiting, and cricked their necks to watch the news on a TV screwed to the ceiling, out of reach.

'Christ,' spat Brendan, at a man being interviewed about his role in Westminster. He was wearing what looked like a lawyer's wig. 'He should be in yer play! Fuckin *wanker*!'

'You're right, actually,' said Martin. The smell of cooking had calmed him somewhat. 'That's exactly what he is. The Remembrancer. He lobbies for the City of London's financial sector.'

'Does he, now?' smirked Brendan. 'The Remembrancer? I'll

no forget *him*!'

When the order was ready, the woman unlocked a small opening in the grille, and passed the mountain of food through, one carton at a time. They were given a pile of carrier bags to transport the feast to the car. Martin was both surprised and relieved when he looked at the hand-written bill, which seemed unbelievably low. 'Keep the change,' he told the woman.

'Okey-dokey,' said Brendan, once they'd settled themselves back into their seats. 'Straight aheid, then first right, second left, and right again at the traffic lights. Got that, Dad?'

'Yes. But would you please put your safety belt on?' asked Martin.

'Whit the fuck dae you care?'

'The alarm. It's doing my head in. Just belt up, would you?'

Brendan obliged, grudgingly, and Martin drove off. 'I've been hi-jacked,' he thought. 'Why can't I think of a way out?' His brain was numb. The car stank of chicken drowning in monosodium glutamate. They reached a dead end – a derelict site. A shed sagged in the headlights, broken windows like mournful eyes, the door clinging to its bottom hinge like a loose tongue.

'This is it,' said Brendan. 'Noo – you cairry in the grub. Ah'll lock up.'

'Look – I'm not a mug either, Brendan,' said Martin, surprising himself with sudden assertiveness, though furious for voluntarily using that stupid name he'd randomly picked. 'I'll carry the food, but I'm keeping the keys.'

To Martin's consternation Brendan grabbed his mobile from the tray where it lay under the dashboard, and using it as a torch, signalled to him to go first. Brendan hauled at the shed door, and Martin stumbled inside, laden like a sherpa with takeaways. Brendan swept the torch over half a dozen cadaverous faces, ranged around a single tea-light that flickered faintly in a jam jar. Discarded syringes glinted here and there on rotting floorboards.

'Party time, ya cunts!' Brendan announced.

A young man signalled to them to be quiet, putting a finger to his broken-toothed mouth – 'Sshhhh!' With the other hand, he waved a bottle of Buckfast above his head. Martin jumped back as the youth smashed it on the ground, and called out 'Tae the deid!' The group, a ghostly chorus, murmured after him: 'Tae the deid… aye – tae the deid.'

'God almighty,' thought Martin. 'Is this some sort of cult?'

'Whit?!' gasped Brendan, as if something had swiped him in the gut. 'Aw naw. Naw. No Jamsie. No ma wee bro. He's never… he's no…?'

'Aye – two hour ago,' replied the Buckfast smasher, without looking up. 'Doon unner the bridge.'

In the half-light of the mobile torch beam, Martin noticed Brendan's face was ash grey – not its former pasty white. He put the bags of food down, but when he straightened himself up, Brendan was gone.

'For god's sake,' thought Martin, feeling his way out of the dark shed and into the yard again, 'he's scarpered with my mobile!' Then he shouted, 'Brendan, you bastard! Come back with my phone!' He pressed the car keys, and the doors clunked, but when he tried to open the driver's side, he realised he must have left the car unlocked when he parked, and had now gone and locked it, because the handle wouldn't release. Calm down, he told himself. Calm DOWN! He clunked again. The door opened this time, and he roared off out of the yard. 'Got to find that bastard – get my bloody phone,' he panted, wildly scanning the pavements and side streets as he drove around, block after block. Under the street lamps, he noticed with horror that his beige trousers were splattered in blood. His heart raced. He touched a spot, and put the finger to his nostrils. Buckfast stains, he realised – of course! – from the spray as the bottle smashed.

*Ting-a-ling, dinga-dinga-dong!* He almost crashed into a bollard, his mobile ring-tone going off somewhere behind him. He pulled in on a quiet side street, and reached into the back, but recoiled in shock. Someone was lying on the seat. He switched on the interior light. It was Brendan, curled up in a foetal position, hugging his knees and rocking.

'What the fuck are you playing at!' Martin snapped, now at the end of his tether. *Ting-a-ling, dinga-dinga-dong!* 'Give me my phone!'

It stopped ringing.

'Ma bro,' moaned Brendan, inconsolable, 'ma bro. Ma wee bro. He's gone an fuckin topped himsel.'

This blade-wielding bandit had turned into a bubbling baby, unaware, it seemed, that his knife now lay on the floor below him. Martin leaned over, picked it up, and slipped it under the mat beneath the driver's seat. His mobile started ringing again, though the sound was muffled, and he couldn't locate it.

'I telt him,' wailed Brendan. 'I telt him no tae dae nuthin stupit. I telt him we'd huv a party, Hogmanay, an aa that. I promised him he'd be OK. But he didnae fuckin listen, did he!' He was shaking now, his whole body racked with sobs.

Martin couldn't think what to do. He'd had nothing to eat since lunch time, his trousers were a mess, the play was about to start, and there was a howling big wean in the back of his car. At least he'd managed to disarm him. He sat in the driver's seat, staring out at the night through trickles of windscreen condensation. At last the sobbing behind him subsided. Brendan appeared to be asleep. 'Should I rouse him?' Martin wondered, thinking he might just be in time to catch the play if he got going now. It was the last night of the run. But did he really want to be hauled through a promenade performance of Scrooge's terrifying visions by actors dressed up as ghosts? He laid his hand on Brendan's shoulder. 'Listen, son,' he said. 'I've got to go home.'

The young man opened his eyes and looked at him blankly: 'Hame?'

Martin thought of his warm cottage, the stove, which he'd stoked before he left, and the rioja waiting on the wine rack. 'Why did that bloke smash the wine bottle on the floor?' he found himself asking, trying to make sense of what he'd seen.

'It's whit we dae. Hameless folk. When wan ae us snuffs it.' Brendan's voice was thin with exhaustion. 'Respect fur the deid.'

'Son,' said Martin, suddenly moved. 'Can I help you? Can I take you somewhere?'

'Naw – ye're OK,' came the reply, almost inaudible.

They sat in silence for a few minutes, cocooned in their own thoughts. Martin leaned over and cleared a patch with his sleeve in the passenger window. There was the sign, nailed to the lamp post – Merryland Street. The evening had come full circle.

'This is where I was born, son – in that gap site, when there was a building there. A nursing home, run by the Sisters of Mercy.'

'Guess it's ma last stop,' said Brendan, sitting up. The mobile dropped to the floor, but he left it there and got out of the car. Mist was seeping in from the Clyde. Martin watched as the young man dragged himself off down the street, and dissolved in the year's last breath.

# The Fiver

FLORA HAD DRIVEN to the Co-op the night before to get change. Two fivers for a ten. She needed the fiver for her daughter Susie, who, due to an extra chromosome, found it difficult to count. Susie felt more confident handing over a note rather than coins in the college canteen. It avoided embarrassment – this way, she could leave it to the cashier to work out the change. A fiver was plenty, Flora felt. Ten ran the risk of overdosing on coke, pizza, custard, chocolate and chips.

The family didn't live near a bank. You had to drive two miles to the nearest shop. There used to be a post office in the village, a tea-room, and a grocer, but that was moons ago. The bus service was dismal, thanks to recent council cuts, so you needed a car, and had to think ahead. Especially when it came to producing a fiver. And Flora was good at that, thinking ahead. Strategy. Anticipating pitfalls. Even more so since her husband's illness. He'd had to stop driving because his brain had taken on the nature of a sieve – routes and landmarks slid through holes into oblivion. He couldn't even remember where the car was parked when they went shopping these days.

Flora was aware that she'd become a carer – that job which happened to other people. She did her best, and people praised her competence, but secretly she felt her head was a tangled mass, like her sewing basket she struggled to keep tidy lately – cotton reels left to unravel, threads not neatly hooked on their notches as they should be, but snagged in a web of blurred colour, nothing distinct.

These thoughts would filter into the front of her brain, but she was good at stitching up the holes they crept through. She wasn't having it. She was lucky, wasn't she? Lived in a beautiful place, had a job that allowed her to work from home. A job she'd always wanted since saving up for her first sewing machine as a girl. She had a good boss who trusted her to come up with rails of stylish clothes that sold in what was generally regarded as the best shop for miles around. And she had flexibility. She'd trained up a small fleet of local cutters and sewers who followed her natty designs. They could keep things going for a while if she got slightly behind.

And she was behind. Things were getting on top of her. That morning she'd set off at six o'clock to pick up her mother in the next village, and drive her forty miles to hospital. Mum's operation would be routine, the doctor said – gall stones, nothing major. But you never knew at that age. For all her ladder-clambering to prune her front door roses, and a mind sharp as secateurs, Mum was nearly ninety.

'I'll be fine,' she said, settling into the passenger seat, and strapping herself in. 'They'll dig them out, and I'll be fine.'

Sounded more like archaeology, thought Flora. 'Don't they smash them inside you, with a laser?'

'Do they? That's a pity. I fancied I'd have mine to keep.'

'Gall stones? What on earth for, Mum?'

'I don't know – teach Susie to count with them? I read somewhere they look like beads,' she said, stroking the spot below her ribs. 'I've a feeling there's quite a lot in there.'

'Damn, damn, *damn it*!' Flora slapped the steering wheel. 'I forgot to give her the fiver!' Then 'Sorry, Mum. Didn't mean to shout.' She didn't want to raise Mum's blood pressure before surgery. But this kind of thing was happening more and more. Seams fraying at the edges. 'Why? Why did I forget' she wailed in her head, not making a sound this time.

Mum rested her hand on Flora's. 'You'll be home before Susie catches her bus. You'll have time to give her the fiver. Relax.'

Her mother's skin was warm. Soft. Deeply familiar. Flora wanted to cry. A whole history in that gesture – all the times they'd ever touched, through childhood, teenage and adult years, the reassurance of her mother's flesh. Like that night before Aunt Isa's funeral, when she was heavily pregnant with Susie, and they'd stayed in a B&B. Flora came out of the shower, and without a word, Mum took hold of the towel and dried her down, gently patting her limbs, her back, her belly. And here they were now, years on, driving together through an autumn dawn, past the loch – trees of yellow and gold mirrored on its still surface. *Red sky at morning, shepherd's warning,* thought Flora. 'I didn't want to just drop you off and leave,' she said. 'I wanted to be with you at the hospital, before they take you into theatre.'

'Not necessary,' replied Mum. 'Get home and make the most of the day. You'll be back in the car to pick me up before you know it.'

But twenty miles on, they hit roadworks, with a sign announcing a diversion.

'They're not letting us go over the bridge, Mum. They're making us take a back road – looks like a one-way system.'

'That road's quicker anyway,' said her mother. 'I always take it when I go for my check-ups. And it's bonnier.'

They drove through a canopy of blazing autumn branches – a fiery tunnel punctuated by one-way blue arrow signs. After a few miles of twists and turns, it opened out onto folding hills, where the hospital appeared to float on rising mist. Mum was happy to be dropped off at the entrance, but Flora went with her to the ward. She wanted to ask about the details of her mother's surgery. Mum winked at the doctor, a young woman who seemed relaxed about it all. 'This daughter of mine's a fuss-pot. She needs reassurance that you're not going to bump me off!'

The diversion signs on the return journey indicated the bridge route. But rush hour traffic was building up by then, and Flora's mobile had just pinged with a text message from Susie: 'I need a fiver, Mum. Dad hasn't got one.' It would be quicker to take the quiet back road from the hospital, even though it had been designated as one way. It wasn't as though there weren't still the two lanes for cars to pass – there were. So, at the roundabout, Flora made the decision. The back road.

Every now and then, as she sped through the tunnel of trees, big red discs confronted her, each with an angry diagonal white strap – the same signs she'd seen en route to the hospital an hour ago, but their reverse sides had faced her then, with blue 'one way' arrows. A car was coming in the opposite direction. She slowed down. The furious driver waved at her wildly, mouthing his rage through a flicker of fiery leaves reflected in his windscreen.

She noticed a farm on the left – access to it along a track, and it occurred to her that the folk living there must have to drive onto the road to get anywhere, and probably did what she was doing. After all, she thought, justifying to herself the choice she'd made, it was only traffic management because of roadworks somewhere else.

Another car approached. She slowed down, and pulled in. The driver gawped at her, making a gun-to-his-head gesture as he passed. It wasn't just the fiver now. A feeling of defiance, of control rose up inside her, the power to strike out alone. There was something about the weather this morning – the sunshine, the blue sky, as if summer had returned unexpectedly. The years fell away, she was a teenager again, life before her. She drove past another three *No Entry* signs.

Music, she thought. Let's have some music. She dug around below the dashboard for her Joni Mitchell greatest hits, and slipped the CD into the player. The spirit of barefoot freedom floated out of the speakers – she could feel the wind blowing in from Africa as she percussed the rhythms on her steering wheel. Her voice swooped with Joni and she was there – heading down to the Mermaid Cafe for one last time with the immortalised Carey and his cane. He had Joni on one arm and herself on the other, and in no time they were toasting their empty glasses to absolutely nothing, and laughing their heads off.

She became aware of a wailing siren outside – distant, though drawing nearer. A police car? Her heart bumped against her ribs. But then the wail ebbed away. Probably an ambulance rushing to the hospital, she decided. She passed the last *No Entry* sign, and reached a T-junction, turned right onto the main carriage-way, and then immediately left along the winding road home, away from diversions at last.

She was singing again – all those places she might go to – Amsterdam, or maybe Rome, her heart-rate normalising, when suddenly, out of nowhere, a police car came screaming up behind her, its blue lights flashing in her rear and wing mirrors. She pulled in and cut Joni dead.

'Where have you come from?' asked the policeman.

She sat in the driver's seat, sick with panic, her window wound down. What if they took her licence away? Her family depended on her to drive them to all kinds of places. She had to pick up her mother later today. She needed the car herself to buy cloth, for deliveries, for the weekly shopping, for a thousand missions stretching ahead of her till doom. She could lie, say she came from that farm she'd spotted on the back road – she remembered its name. She looked into the policeman's face. His features weren't harsh.

'I'm asking where you've come from.'

She had a sudden urge to say 'The Mermaid Café', but thought better of it. 'The hospital,' she sighed, her head sinking into her chest.

Another policeman, younger and taller than the one asking questions, was taking notes. Just a skinny lad, enjoying wearing his uniform, she could tell. He looked up from his smartphone to check out the details of her car, the ragged wheel trims, mud splatters on the doors. It's nearly as old as him, she thought, as he logged the registration number.

'And how many *No Entry* signs have you driven past?' asked the older man.

She knew it was at least six: 'Three or four?' she offered.

He didn't contradict her. 'Quite a few drivers passed you. They were raging. Couldn't believe it. Have you any idea of the risk you were taking?'

'Let's see your licence,' said the young man. But she noticed the older one checking him with a glance. *I'm dealing with this,* his eyes said.

She fumbled in her bag for her purse, and fished out the ancient, folded scrap of pink paper. 'Sorry – it's not the new kind, I mean the proper card thingy... it's just, I haven't got round to applying... I think I'll get out of the car, if you don't mind. Take some air.'

She stood on the roadside, feeling small in her simple grey dress. She thought of it as a comfortable classic, and was wearing it in honour of Mum who liked it. But right now it made her feel like a schoolgirl.

'You see,' she explained in a sudden flood, 'I had to take my mother to hospital – my husband doesn't drive, his memory's shredded – and I have to get back home to give my daughter a fiver before she sets off for college, because she has an extra chromosome and can't count, so it's easier for her in the canteen if she doesn't have to add coins, and there were all those roadworks, a diversion, and I thought the back road would be quicker – I didn't drive fast, I was careful, but yes. Yes. You're right. I was wrong. And now I'll be too late with the fiver anyway. So I was very wrong.'

The men were silent. Perhaps they didn't believe her.

'You can come home if you like, and meet my family – see for yourself.'

She watched them as they moved towards their own car, talking quietly, so that she couldn't hear. She might be taken to a police cell. They'd fingerprint her, she supposed, and photograph her – a criminal against a wall, looking straight at the lens.

An unexpected calm descended on her, a kind of Doris Day moment – *que sera sera*. Anything can happen to anyone, she thought, and it's happening to me, a story unfolding, and I'm in it, no matter what.

The older policeman walked back to her.

'The thing is,' he said meaningfully, his brown eyes looking right into hers, 'we didn't see you driving on or out of that one-way road. We only saw you turning into this one.' He seemed to be trying to get her to understand something.

The young lad scuffed the toe of his boot on the road. His whole body expressed more than disappointment, something verging on disgust.

'So,' continued the older man, 'because we didn't actually see you, we're not going to charge you.'

'Thank you,' she said, barely voicing the words. 'Thank you.'

'Mind, now,' he replied, gently matching her quietness. 'It's a warning.'

She stood still for a moment as they drove off. The sun had risen above the hills, like a good omen. A reprieve. She breathed in a lung-full of morning, the tang of damp leaves and dewy grass in her throat. As she climbed back into the car, her phone pinged with a text message. It was Susie again: 'I've got a fiver left from my birthday money. I'm going for the bus. It's all fine.'

And somehow the familiar guddle of gall stones, chromosomes, and lost memory files seemed peculiarly comforting. 'Mum was right,' thought Flora, 'I still have the whole day ahead. Time to tackle the fankled contents of that sewing box, and get cracking on the back-log of orders.'

She turned the key in the ignition, and headed home.

# The Grail

SLEET DROVE THROUGH the Edinburgh dusk. The gutters ran like rivers. Rhona already felt she was hauling her body through accumulated piles of slush – she didn't need the weather to rub it in: the effort of trying to get going again after the onslaught of the Festive Season, bracing herself for 'pitching' ideas to funders and publishers, steeling herself against the inevitable rejections. 'Pitching'. She hated that term, lovely once, when it meant what you did with tents. Or singing. The prospect of another year made her think about the trail of time she'd left behind, and only increased the piles of slush ahead, which were literal now, as she slipped about on pavements in the half-light, traffic splattering icy water at her ankles.

Why she'd decided to roll up at a preview in this weather was beyond her. And she was too early – didn't need to be there for at least another hour. Jen would have understood if she'd called off – they were old pals – and in any case, the exhibition would be on for a month. The bus home might not be running if this sleet turned to snow. And the temperature was definitely falling. Still, she was here now – better make the best of it: find a coffee shop, and read her book.

A few decades ago this would have been an adventure – getting stuck in town for the night. Like the time she missed the last bus home on Christmas Eve. It was her final year at school, and she'd come into town to meet up with her boyfriend at his bedsit near the art college where he was studying. All planned – her 'first time'. She'd even got herself sorted with The Pill. Mrs Darnley, his landlady, leaned over the bannister, nailing Rhona with her eyes as she climbed the tenement stairwell to the third landing, the unknown drawing closer with each step.

'A cold night for it,' nipped Mrs D of the floral pinnie and switchblade tongue, implying 'it' was something illicit. Nevertheless, she held the front door open for Rhona, who blushed in the bare light bulb and linoleum glare. The reek of chip fat turned her stomach. Mrs D's eyes narrowed: 'Your young man's in his room.'

The blare of a car horn sent Rhona skiting along the icy pavement into a passer-by. 'Sorry!' she gasped. 'So sorry!'

The man gripped her elbow and steadied her with a gloved hand. 'Need yer wits about you in this weather!'

'Do you know where The Grail is?' she asked him. 'It used to be somewhere near here, through a door and up a stair.'

'Ye're in a dwam, wumman. This is Edinburgh – no Camelot!'

'There *was* a place near here – coffee and books. But I've been away for years.'

'There's a Starbucks a few doors down that way,' he nodded, and walked off into a veil of sleet.

She might have been in a dwam, but not about The Grail. How could she ever forget it? A honeycomb of rooms lined with books and hessian wallpaper, and floorboards that creaked amiably under rush matting. Bach or Mozart caressed the air gently enough for conversation, and the coffee aroma enveloped you like a comfort blanket. Deliciously moist date and walnut cake was served on wooden plates. You could sit in an ample armchair, and read books without buying them – no-one bothered you. Rhona did buy one, though – for him, that Christmas Eve – *The Rubaiyat of Omar Khayyam*, and took it with her to his room at Mrs D's, a gift to mark their moment. It was sleeting then too, and turned to snow. By the time they'd done their loving, sleeping and waking, the city was a new landscape, still and silent as a Christmas card. His first Scottish Noel, far from Italy. They'd missed the last bus, and cooried into a freezing phone box to let her parents know they'd be late, would take a corporation bus to the outskirts, and walk home from there. It was several miles, and blood trickled down her legs. She hadn't known this would happen – no-one had told her she had a hymen. But he reassured her, giving her a wadge of tissue hankies to stuff into her pants. They laughed and sang carols, their voices pealing over moonlit snow fields.

Rhona sat in Starbucks at a metallic plastic table, and caught sight of herself in a large mirror. She should have gone to the hairdresser – grey was edging through at her temples again. But living out in the country now, sitting at her desk all day, drawing, she tended to forget about her appearance. And work left her with little time for anything other than managing day-to-day family arrangements. New clothes and hairdressing were a low priority. She looked into the mirror again. It wasn't just her temples. The harsh lighting picked up the grey all along her parting. She shifted the chair to turn her back on the offending reflection, and sipped her lukewarm cappuccino. It was a bucket-sized cup, absurdly big for the 'medium' she'd ordered, and wrapping her hands round its girth did nothing to get the blood circulating again. Her table was near to the door, which swung open as customers came and went, snaring her in the street's icy blast. Oh, for the long-lost Grail…

She met him there one Saturday. She and a pal had gone into town for the day. It was Puccini and Leoncavallo that morning

– not the usual Mozart or Bach – because he was in charge – his weekend job. He hummed the arias behind the oak counter in a cloud of steam from the coffee machine. Everything about him was easy, natural, his open smile, the candid, petrol-blue eyes under a mop of lawless black curls. 'Vitale!' she heard the owner call from one of the other rooms. Vitale…

That summer, they climbed Scald Law, one of the Pentland Hills. He took his camera to capture lichens, moss and stone for a student assignment. She sweated all the way, wearing tights under her jeans, in case he tried anything, which he did, as they lay down on a grassy slope. She needn't have worried, though, because he didn't persist – just leapt up onto the Ordnance Survey trig pillar, and sang out like Caruso to the whole Pentland range: *Ridi, Pagliaccio! My girl she just said No! No! O, ridi, Pagliaccio!* That made her laugh so much she almost changed her mind, but was glad she didn't. Glad they waited till the snow came…

Another icy blast from Starbuck's doorway was too much, so she moved to an empty table round a corner, with more protection. But the crumbs, coffee puddles and screwed up paper napkins were off-putting, so she paid for her unfinished cappuccino, and went back out onto the street. The cold had made her hungry. There was still time enough for a quick bite. Across the road, a trattoria glowed through snowfall, windows and door looped with red and yellow lanterns. That would do. She held onto a handrail, stepping gingerly down the slushy steps. A dapper young man in waistcoat and tie opened the door for her:

'Benvenuta, signora!'

An older man, dressed in a similar outfit, though with tie loosened and shirt collar open, was smiling at her, arms held out in welcome.

'Rhona!'

'Em... do I... do I know you?' she asked, stamping the snow from her shoes.

'You do,' he laughed.

Who was this chubby, middle-aged waiter, a stranger, behaving so familiarly? 'I'm sorry. I don't. I think you're confusing me with someone else.'

'Never,' he said, 'You look just the same.'

By now the whole restaurant was watching. All conversation had stopped. He didn't move, just stood, waiting, and gave a forlorn smile as her eyes fell on his middle-aged spread. She summoned all her powers of recall, examining his features intensely for something recognisable, the curly grey hair, the blue eyes – those surprisingly candid, petrol-blue eyes. 'Vitale! Vitale!! How *are* you?'

'Glad to see you...' he smiled.

'Old boyfriend, old girlfriend!' called one of the waiters behind the bar, and everyone clapped and cheered.

'Do you still live here? What about your photography? Are you married?' her questions tumbled out in a shameless spate, the years frothing and bubbling up through every word.

'Yes, yes, I got married,' he said quietly, as if to calm her. 'I have a son.'

'Happy? I hope you're happy.'

'Oh, you know – so-so,' he joked with a rocking hand gesture. 'Come on. Let's sit down.'

The other waiters fluttered about with cloths, cutlery, glasses, setting the table for them, while customers resumed their conversations.

'But don't you have to work now?' she asked.

'It's OK. We're not so busy.' He took a zippo from his pocket – she remembered that zippo, with its Venetian scrolled leaves.

'Anyway,' he smiled, lighting a candle, 'this isn't every day, is it!'

'You mean us?'

'Yes, of course!' He clicked shut the flame. 'And Burns Night. We've put on a special menu – haggis, the works!'

'I forgot it was Burns Night.' The realisation dismayed her. 'I've been away too long.'

'The weather's put people off,' he said. 'But that's good – means I'm not needed at the tables.'

They ordered chianti, and raised their glasses.

'I read about you in the papers,' he told her, 'your books. I follow you.'

She detected something subdued in his tone. Quiescent. Resigned, even. 'Do you remember The Grail?' she asked. 'I was trying to find it today, but it's not there any more.'

'You won't find something that doesn't exist,' he said, making a sad clown face in the candlelight.

'It did, though, Vitale!' She loved saying his name again after all those years. 'The Grail was there! *We* were there – you singing your arias.'

'I was doing this job even then!' he groaned.

'Omar Khayyam – do you remember? I bought *The Rubaiyat* for you there.'

'I still have it,' he said. 'beautiful illustrations – golden sunsets and dawns.'

'Dulac. The master – it was quite a sacrifice for me, giving it to you!'

'*A loaf of bread, a jug of wine, and Zou.*'

'Yes – you couldn't say your *ths* back then! I used to love that!'

The rush of excitement in meeting ebbed, and they dined with quiet intimacy, catching up on the years. He told her how he'd moved from photographing landscapes to people, but it didn't work out. 'I discovered I wasn't Diane Arbus', was how he put it.

'Maybe you just haven't found the right subject, or the best lens to look through?'

'Too late. I've become a cliché – an Italian waiter.'

'That's a British cliché. Nothing to do with you, Vitale.'

'You did the right thing to live in the world of children with your art, Rhona – those gorgeous fantasies you paint in your books. The adults dried me up.'

'The ones I have to deal with dry me up too.'

'But you've made a success of what you do, without compromising your art,' he said.

'It's still hard, though' she replied. 'Harder than ever. There's no loyalty out there. Boy, do I appreciate the time I spent studying.' She told him about her student days, training in London, then Poznan and Berlin, getting married back in London, bringing up their child, and now returning home with her husband. 'When you think about it,' she said, savouring the first clapshot she'd tasted in years, 'you're more Scottish than I am. All the time I've been away, you've been here, what – two thirds of your life?'

'I suppose so. I came here and stayed. You escaped.'

'Escaped? You always loved Scotland, Vitale.'

'I did, I do –'

'The landscape got under your skin – that's what you used to say.'

'Yes, but everything's changing now,' he said, with a weary sigh. 'Everything's franchised. Like this place, and I don't know if I'll be able to stay much longer – I'm not British. And anyway, my son's moved to Germany. My turn to escape.'

'And your wife?'

'It didn't last.'

He reached out across the table, touching her grey temples.

'Nor does my hair colour these days,' she joked, avoiding his eyes. Silly, she knew, but at that moment she wanted to look her best for him, wanted *now* to be *then*, for time to roll back.

'And your husband?' he asked.

'Oh, you know – we keep the show on the road.'

Cranachan was served, followed by a dram. He lifted his glass and clinked hers. 'For auld lang syne,' he smiled.

'Canta per noi *Una Red, Red Rose*, Vitale!' called one of the waiters.

'Canta! Canta, Vitale!' the others joined in.

'Go on,' Rhona coaxed, 'I'd love to hear you sing again.'

He stood up, drew in his belly with elaborate self-deprecation, making her laugh – that sad *pagliaccio* he'd played for her decades ago on Scald Law – and then sang, the same pure tenor voice:

> *Il mio amore è una rosa rossa*
> *che in giugno si schiude;*
> *il mio amore è una melodia*
> *suonata dolcemente.*

It didn't quite scan, but somehow he lengthened Burns' phrasing, and made it all his own. Everyone applauded, and he sat down again, taking her hands in his.

'Would you look at the time!' she exclaimed, catching sight of his watch. The other tables were empty, the last of the customers leaving. 'We've been here for hours! I was going to a preview – a friend's exhibition...'

'Oh – I've held you up,' he apologised.

'No, I don't want to move from this chair *ever*. But –'

'I know,' he interrupted, with a glint of recognition, 'you

might miss the last bus home?'

Was this an invitation, she wondered? He fetched her coat and held it open for her.

'I've got ten minutes,' she said, fastening the buttons. 'I can catch it at the stop just along from The Grail.'

'But there is no Grail,' he reminded her.

'There is tonight,' she said. 'I found it when I walked in here.'

He led her to the door.

'Buona notte, Signora!' called the other waiters.

'Grazie,' she waved to them. 'Grazie mille!'

Snow had fallen heavily all evening. They stood on the steps, holding hands, hushed, like the city itself. She didn't know how to leave him, how to let go of the past they'd just reclaimed. He kissed her on the cheek, then said, 'Now go.'

'Old girlfriend! Old boyfriend!' the waiters' voices reprised behind the closed door as she walked away, their laughter fading on the frosted air.

Three weeks later, Rhona was facing up to the new year. The evenings were lengthening, and she went into town to catch Jen's exhibition. Crocuses were out all along The Meadows. Her step was light. She'd taken an early bus, and had time to spare. She crossed the street to the trattoria, but found herself disorientated – its name had changed: *The Albion*. A man was up a ladder, scrubbing out some letters that looked as though they'd been spray-painted above the new name. She could just make out the word he was erasing – *Perfidious*. The lanterns around the windows and door had gone. But the steps to the entrance were there, the handrail, the same brass door handle. The interior was newly decorated – a cool, corporate style. Gone the rustic red table cloths, with candles set in their straw-swaddled chianti bottles. A tall woman, sharp-edged in high heels approached Rhona from the back of the restaurant.

'Do you have a reservation, madam?'

'No. I'm looking for someone. Vitale.'

'Vitale?' The woman's eyes were blank.

'Yes, he works here,' said Rhona.

'Not any more. The staff's changed – a new franchise.'

'Do you have a contact for him?'

'No. I'm afraid not.'

Rhona stepped back outside. What had she expected, even if he'd been there today? Their moment was in the past. She supposed that's why they hadn't offered to exchanged phone numbers. They both had 'lives to live', whatever that meant, though she was troubled by what might be happening to his. Was he still in the city, alone, perhaps, without work? Or was he no longer welcome here, his only option to leave? *Perfidious Albion*. What did that phrase mean? It had an antique ring to it, historical, something to do with treachery, she thought.

She walked along the street towards the gallery, glancing up at the vanished Grail. Change. We have to embrace it, she told herself, 'pitching', 'bidding', moving forward. The way of the world. But she felt uneasy. Increasingly uneasy.

# A Botanical Curiosity for Eve

FIRST IT WAS the pandemic. If it was over. Who could be sure? She still wore a mask when she went shopping. Just in case. It had been so bleak, holed up at home with her husband for months on end. They'd never spent so much time together, though they'd been married for over twenty years. During the first lockdown, conversation petered out, and they started to sleep separately.

Then he left. And now, due to one thing and another – her euphemism for prosecco – it had happened again – she'd lost a commission, the third this year. And it was only April.

She'd always felt she was on the back foot. No-one had ever understood her. She wasn't even sure she understood herself. Her daughter wasn't unsupportive, but her last words when she left to go back to uni weren't exactly comforting: 'Keep your chin up, Mum! Remember – you're in control!'

Control? When had she ever had any of *that*? If there was justice out there, she'd be properly acknowledged by now. She hadn't quite made Gold with her gardens at the Chelsea Flower Show, but she'd proved she was top of the tree. Just look at what she'd achieved with her arbours, pergolas and belvederes. She had 'a distinctive way of coaxing magic from the natural world'. That's what a well-known journalist had written about her in a leading feature for a weekend colour supplement – a big splash, it was. Though you could hardly call it recent.

'Face it, Eve. Your client pool has gone seriously down-market,' her husband had liked to remind her – even before the pandemic. And now, because of damned Covid, people had got into the habit of Do-It-Yourself.

It didn't help that her father – the late, great illustrious 'pater', a globe-trotting absence most of her life – had occupied similar territory: the ground-breaking Alaskan botanist, whose specimens were in botanical gardens all over the planet. 'Oh, you're the daughter of' was the panel's opening gambit at so many dreary job interviews, and the predictable tag when people – invariably men – introduced her to anyone who might be important. Yes, as she knew to her cost, Adam was the gardener, and Eve carried his trowel.

She picked up her phone and dialled a number.

'Is that Seb – the gardening handy-man?'

'That's me.'

'I saw your advert in the Co-op.'

'Oh, aye.'

'I'm needing some work done – quite a bit, actually. My old gardener moved away, and I've let things slip, what with one thing and another.' She reached for the fridge door and lifted out a bottle. 'A total overhaul, in fact. Would you be up for that?'

'I could come and have a look.'

His voice was deep and woody. Nice, she thought, pouring herself a glass.

'Where d'ye stay?'

She gave him the address, and then her name.

'Not Eve Brechin, the daughter of –'

Here we go, she thought, then chirped: 'Yes. That's me!'

She put him in her diary – only a couple of days to wait. God knows what she was going to pay him with, but she'd work it out. She still had some credit on one of her bank cards, and the online consultations were slowly picking up. There was no choice, in any case. She couldn't bear to look out from the kitchen at the eyesore her garden had become. It was paradise once, a haven of peace in the bustle of the city. That is, before her husband appropriated it for his work. An events manager – a dashingly handsome, charming fast talker, always jetting about for one corporate group or another. The most miraculous event he'd ever managed was getting her pregnant, given he was away so much. That was her bitter little joke. Every few months he'd return home, only to set everything in a whirl, the garden throbbing with elaborate preparations for his clients' entertainment – illuminations and large digital screens, totally at odds with the space she'd created. He assured her that these events would spread interest in her skills among people with influence, a joint investment, so to speak. But they never yielded anything.

She opened the French windows that led from the sitting room onto the terrace, and stood there for a moment, sipping prosecco, weighing up the work ahead. Three years of neglect had resulted in botanical havoc, weeds spreading viciously between the paving stones. The lawn was more like a hayfield – she hoped Seb had a strimmer. The walls, pathways and raised beds crawled with nettles and dockens, and the greenhouse looked pitifully woebegone, its panes cracked and streaked with moss. The woven willow sitooterie – her daughter's favourite bolt-hole – was beginning to sag next to the lily pond. And the straggling broom bush, which, for some strange reason, had no buds this year, fluttered last autumn's pods at her like tiny black flags.

It was one of those perfect afternoons. Rare these days. The sun was shining, barely a breeze, the sky delphinium blue. She'd just taken the prosecco out of the fridge – why not? A wee toast to a new working relationship would set things off on the right track. And there he was – Seb, a tall, clean-shaven young man with long auburn hair tied in a ponytail, surveying the garden. He must have let himself in at the gate. She opened the French windows and took two softly fizzing glasses out onto the terrace, a strawberry perched on each rim.

'Hello, there!' she hallooed – a little too excitedly, she noticed to her dismay – and handed him a glass.

'Thanks, but I'm afraid I don't drink.'

'Oh, well,' she sighed extravagantly, throwing off the rejection with mock disappointment, 'I'll just have to take care of them both!'

They waded through weeds while she explained what was required and he made notes in a small book. He was particularly attracted to the well in the centre of the garden, with its dry-stane wall.

'That used to be the local water supply in the old days. Part of what attracted me to the house when I moved in,' she told him, editing her husband from the story. 'So I decided to keep it there.'

'It's a bonnie feature,' he agreed.

By the time she'd drained the second glass, she was laying out her vision for a complete revamp of the whole space. Apart from the well, which would remain, of course.

'First things first,' Seb cautioned, putting the notebook back in his shirt pocket. 'The weather's that unpredictable lately. Crazy extremes. Let's see how we go.'

'I'll do a sketch for you if you like,' she smiled, 'an Eve Brechin special!'

'Aye, well – no harm.'

'Exactly. And you can have a look at it when you come next time. I've a feeling you're the kind of man who likes a challenge.'

Why was it, she wondered, sitting alone on the sofa that evening – why couldn't she get the tone right when it came to men?

She frequently embarrassed herself, but she'd never admit it to anyone. There wasn't a chink in her armour, although it was brittle as eggshell. She'd been flirting with Seb, ridiculous at her age, she knew. He was almost young enough to be her son. She'd probably managed to put him right off. Although when they spoke on the phone initially, he seemed interested. He'd recognised her name straight away, even if it was because of her father. But maybe pater's ghost was her insurance in this case, and would bring Seb back.

Something made her go into the attic that night. She got the ladder out, and in a poignant prosecco haze, swayed up the rungs and into the past. Her torch swept through the darkness picking out crates of old toys, and the family cot she'd slept in as a baby – as had her own daughter – its pink paint scratched and flaking – abandoned fragments of lives that had moved on. And boxes of her father's papers, valuable material she intended to sort out in preparation for selling to the Royal Botanics for their archive, but the task was too much and she'd given up. Mice droppings peppered the floor boards. Her torch beam caught the chewed edge of a bag, which must have fallen, or perhaps had been dragged from its box. The contents – a series of black and white photographs – were strewn across the floor. She panicked for a moment. As his only child, her father's papers were her responsibility. Her parents had divorced, and Mum, now in a care home, never expressed any interest in them. Why should she? It would have helped, though, to have someone with knowledge go through the stuff, give her a few sign posts – so much of it was from before her time. But Mum's memory was shot to pieces. Eve felt she'd lost her entirely since the care home became a prison during Covid, when no-one was permitted to visit. Just agonising glimpses at the window, Mum waving like a frail ghost from another world...

Eve gathered the strewn photos, and leafed through them: men lined up at conferences and award ceremonies, handshakes and toasts; her father in the Arctic tundra, proudly holding a specimen of some plant or other. And one of him sitting by a river. He was looking up at a tall bearded man who was standing on top of a rock, roaring with laughter. Her heart started to race, blood thundered in her head. That face, that beard, that fierce laugh suddenly engulfed the attic.

She'd been let out of high school early to catch the bus into the city. Her father had arranged it. She was going to join his friend, the bearded professor and his students at the Royal Botanics. An educational opportunity. But first on the menu was lunch at his house. She was sweating so much with nerves, her finger slipped on the doorbell. Why hadn't she thought of bringing a change of clothes? She would look so conspicuous and silly among the students, dressed in her school uniform. She could feel his footsteps reverberating through the vestibule, as he approached the door.

'Eve – my little scholar!' he boomed, and scooped her up in a bear hug. Lunch wasn't quite ready, he said, leading her into a bay-windowed room, flooded with sunlight. It was too bright, he said, drawing the curtains. And then the experiment. That's what he called it. He told her to lie on the floor and imagine her body was the earth itself. Seeds taking root in her, like Adam's rib, green shoots rising – could she feel it? He removed his tie, then hers, unbuttoned her white school shirt, and lay down beside her. Next thing he had her bra off, wheezing through his beard, scraping its prickles across her breasts, his fingers fishing around under her skirt, into her tights and pants. She was staring at the rose in the centre of the pale, corniced ceiling, when she heard the front door open.

Wiping his crotch with his hand, he scrambled to his feet, zipped up his flies, and left the room. She'd just about got her clothes back on, when his beard came round the door, and the words, 'Lunch is ready!' slid out of the pink mouth.

His pretty wife, blonde and silent, stood at the mahogany dining table, serving. 'Pussy makes the best Hungarian goulash,' he gushed, gravy dripping down the beard. She'd never tasted the dish before, and never did again.

There was a scurry in the attic. She swung the torch and caught sight of a mouse vanishing into the shadows. She took another look at the photo, and with deliberate precision, tore it down the middle, right through the centre of the laughing beard, the torso, the crotch, and the rock. Her father was left on the river bank looking up at only half a man, which struck her as terribly funny. She wished she'd brought the prosecco up here with her – she could do with another glass, if only to toast the beard's demise.

She placed the two halves of the photo in her pocket. 'Compost,' she thought, gleefully. Then she stuffed the rest of the photos into their nibbled bag. As she put it back in the box, her torch beam picked out an envelope, bearing her own name in her father's copperplate hand: *A botanical curiosity for Eve.* It was sealed. Had he forgotten to give it to her? Or had he intended she should find it? She put that in her pocket too, and climbed out of the attic.

Back in the sitting room, she curled up on the sofa and poured another glass. Then she took out the envelope. There was a miniature parcel in it, and a letter:

*Eve – I found this curiosity in a long-lost ghost ship, which I boarded with some natives on the Bering Sea. One of them said he knew what it was, but I somehow doubt it. At any rate, he wouldn't tell me. The only seed I've never been able to identify. I often thought of planting it, to see what might grow, but for some unknown reason, kept it as a talisman. You might as well have it as any, given that you seem to be navigating my territory. So here you are, now it's yours, gifted to you 'from the other side', as they say. Pater.*

She unwrapped the parcel's yellowing tissue paper to find a small glass phial containing what looked like a single dark seed. She took out her magnifying glass from the bureau, and tipped the seed into her palm. She couldn't decide whether it was heart-shaped – a miniature version of those sea beans from South America that get washed down river into the ocean and land on a distant shore – or, depending on the angle at which it lay in her palm, a tiny cloven hoof.

A few days later, she was tidying up in the greenhouse, listening to the radio, when Seb appeared with his strimmer.

He waved and called to her, 'Thought I'd make a start!'

She resisted the desire to rush out and greet him – just waved back cheerily. She watched his body sway back and forth with easy grace as he swept the blade across the straggling weeds. In a few hours the garden was almost a blank canvas.

'Marvellous,' she enthused, and handed him her sketch, complete with a colour-coded key at the foot showing the list of plants she envisaged.

'Well,' he said, wiping the sweat from his face and neck, 'it'll need a lot of digging in the beds. But like you said the last time, I'm up for a challenge.'

'I take it that's a 'Yes'?' she twinkled.

'Aye.' Then, looking more carefully at her sketch he added:

'I can see it'll be bonnie, and a riot o colour. Only thing is, am I right thinkin the whole thing's goin to be poison?'

'Oh? I'm not sure I was conscious of that!' she bluffed, reddening at being rumbled. 'Anyway, it won't be a garden for eating – strictly for looking.'

'It'll need tae come wi a health warnin,' he said, packing away his gear and glancing up at the sky. 'Weird colour the day. The chief and his cronies must be on the ozone gin again.'

Summer came in. Life felt more focused now that she had a goal of sorts, even if, as she admitted to herself, it was some vague form of revenge. She made a bit of money from a couple of third-rate commissions and paid Seb, who seemed content to carry out her instructions. He was a hard worker and clearly had a lot of knowledge. A breath of fresh air, she thought, whenever he turned up. But he kept to himself, and she regretted his lack of interest in her. The garden was taking shape, though. It was going to be better than anything ever seen in Chelsea. Not that she was bothered about the public. This one was exclusively for herself.

She'd been wondering what to do with her father's 'talisman'. Eventually curiosity got the better of her. She selected a clay pot in the greenhouse, filled it with compost, and emptied the tiny seed from the glass phial into her palm. Seb appeared at the door.

'What have ye got there, eh?'

'Not sure,' she replied. 'Unidentified.'

'Strange shape fur a seed,' he said, peering at it. 'Where did ye get it?'

'A gift from the grave, you might say.'

'Yer father?'

'It's decades old,' she said, avoiding his question. She didn't want to talk about pater. 'I can't imagine it'll grow.'

'Is it poisonous?' he asked.

'I don't know. I shouldn't think so.'

'The only safe bet in the garden, then!' he laughed, as she dropped it into the little hole she'd made in the compost, and covered it over with her finger.

Every day, first thing, she'd check its progress. It sprouted within a week – clearly the humidity and sunlight of the greenhouse was the perfect environment. Shoots appeared on the strong stem, growing rapidly into thick copper-coloured, spiky leaves, with an intense, musky aroma. In no time at all it was a small sapling, which she transplanted outside in the sunniest spot at the centre of the garden, beside the old well.

Summer wore on. She wasn't sleeping well, and her prosecco sessions weren't lessening, in spite of her promises to cut down.

'I'm not coming home over the holidays to put up with you being pissed, Mum,' her daughter had said during a phone call at the end of term.

After a string of sleepless nights, she got up at dawn and climbed the ladder to the attic again. She'd decided to bring down her father's boxes, not with the Royal Botanics in mind, but a bonfire. If the contents were sold, the money wouldn't come to her anyway. It would go straight to her mother's account, only to be sucked into the funds paying the care home bills. She went out to the garden in her nightdress, and emptied the boxes onto the spot Seb used for burning refuse. The light breeze was just enough to get the flames going. Sheaves of academic papers curled red and then blackened. Photos fluttered about as if trying to escape the inferno. One of them did, its smoking edge almost brushing the hem of her nightie, but as the breeze dropped, it drifted to the ground. There at her feet was the house where she was born, the street where she'd played, and on the corner, the news agent's. Even although the photo, decades old, was monochrome, and beginning to melt with the heat, the shop's striped awning – pink and white like its wrinkled owner – stamped itself on her retina.

She was waiting in the front shop to begin her pocket money job, the Saturday morning paper round. His hungry smile flashed at her, as he brought the stack of newspapers round from behind the counter, and packed them for her into the canvas bag slung over her shoulder. He pressed against her, popping sweets into her mouth, his other hand making its way up her skirt. And between the sweet-popping, from under the magazines piled on the counter, he pulled out front covers of naked women with ballooning breasts, their nipples glistening like bubble gum. His wife was shouting for him, banging her walking sticks as she hobbled into view, black hair pulled into a tight bun, every strand gripping her waxy, red-lipped face, a tarantula advancing from the back shop.

'Off you go, then, wee Eve!' he chirped, smacking her bum as he slipped the bare-breasted women back under the *Scottish Field*.

A pale, sickly sun rose above the laburnum, and the bonfire died down. She was still standing there in her nightdress an hour later, staring at the ashes, when Seb came through the gate.

'You OK?' he asked.

She walked straight past him without looking, went back to bed and lay there, exhausted, until sleep came.

When she woke, she felt a weight had lifted. For the first time, the empty wine glass on her bed-side table affronted her, and she decided to cancel the latest case of prosecco she'd ordered. She got up and looked down onto the garden from her bedroom window. Seb was bent over, pulling weeds from among the lupins. He never wanted anything from her, just got on with what was needed. She liked having him around. The first man she'd ever really felt comfortable with. And the garden was beautiful. Just as she'd envisaged. But somehow its theme seemed absurd now, pointless, and no longer held any appeal.

She watched as he pushed a wheel barrow full of weeds over to the refuse pile, where the ashes lay. He caught sight of her at the upstairs window and waved. She waved back. On his return with the empty barrow, he stopped at the well.

The strange tree was thriving there, its growth phenomenally fast – almost as tall as Seb. The branches were covered in large blooms, five petals to each one, all cloven-shaped like the seed. Their colour altered at different times of day. In the morning, when the buds opened, the petals were lilac. Right now, at midday, they were somewhere between purple and maroon, and at dusk deepened to midnight blue. They were beginning to fade, leaving shining black berries.

She got dressed, and went down to the garden with her secateurs, thinking she might cut a few of the last blooms before they withered, and put them in a vase.

'Did you get some rest?' asked Seb.

'Yes, thanks. I did.'

'This is the weirdest tree I've ever seen. Eldritch,' he murmured, feeling the leathery leaves. 'That's what my grandad would've called it – eldritch.'

He picked a berry and held it to his nose. 'Some scent, though! Like vanilla, but more musky.' And he took a bite.

'Don't!' Eve gasped. 'It might not be edible!'

'It's OK,' he said, spitting it out into the well. 'I didn't swallow. Just a tiny bit of the skin. It's delicious.'

She rushed into the house and came running back with a large glass of water. 'Drink!' she insisted. 'Drink all of it – now!'

'Alright,' he laughed, 'if it makes you feel better,' and downed the lot to oblige her.

'Seb,' she said, taking the empty glass from him, 'I know you've put in all this work, and it's looking gorgeous – the colours, the shapes, the scents – everything. But next Spring let's dig it all up, start afresh and make another garden. Roses and honeysuckle, anything you like.'

He looked bewildered. 'I thought poison was your thing. And I was gettin used to bein yer partner in crime!'

The next day, he texted to say he needed to take a break. He'd be back in touch soon. She waited for a fortnight, but heard nothing. There was no answer when she called his phone. On the radio in the greenhouse, she heard news of a strange sickness spreading like wildfire. She wasn't feeling too well herself. She tried to ring her daughter, and her mother in the care home, but couldn't get through, so she left voice-mail messages for them both. Then she put on her mask, and went round to the Co-op to ask for Seb. But it was closed.

Shops were shuttered all along the street. Autumn had barely established itself, yet snowflakes were falling, blanketing the silent pavement and road. The jaundiced yellow tinge had returned to the sky, and reminded Eve of her mother's paper-thin skin.

In the garden, though its leathery leaves still remained, the eldritch tree – that's what she called it now – had shed all its berries. Perhaps birds had eaten them, or maybe they'd fallen into the well. The scent seemed more intense than ever, but with a bitter edge. It caught her breath, as if the bark and leaves were exhaling, releasing clouds of invisible, acrid sap into her lungs. She'd have to find an axe and bring it down.

# Skeleton Wumman

*You went astray*
*among the mysterious foliage of the sea-bottom*
*in the green half-light without love...*

*you in the half-light of your sleep*
*haunting the bottom of the sea without ceasing*
*and I hauling and hauling on the surface.*

(From '*Tha thu air Aigeann m' Inntinn*'/
'You Are At The Bottom of My Mind'
Iain Crichton Smith, *New Collected Poems*, Carcanet Press)

IT WIS CAULD doon there. Suited me. Sae cauld I could haurdly think nor feel. Nae skin tinglin like sea anemones, nae pink fronds that thrilled tae the touch, just banes, stripped o flesh, white an free o pain. That wis me, Skeleton Wumman, a rickle o banes, riddlin the waves wi ma fingers an taes. Aa ma jynts in guid workin order, visible tae the myriad fish, but hidden frae fowk up there – them that micht be left... ma faither, ma mither. They could be onywhaur, efter whit happened, onywhaur...

I've nae idea hoo lang I wis doon there. Days? Months? Could hae been years. I dinnae ken whit time *is* ony mair. I hud a strange feelin, though, in ma banes that somethin wis gonnae happen. I ken that's whit folk aye say, but in *ma* case, whaur else could I feel?!

I never slept, but I wisnae awauk neethur, in a hauf state o bein, hingin aboot, clinkin agin cockles an cowries that driftit like snaw. Noo an then I'd hear the kirk bell dunnelin. Would hae been when the tide wis low, I suppose, the belfry risin ower the waves – must hae looked like a submarine! I could hear it frae doon there on the sea flair, muffled, a ringin happed in mist. Mibbe it wis a dolphin wi a sense o humour pullin the rope, or mibbe just the wecht o the watter giein a tug. But it happened, ilka low tide. 'Lang syne, lang syne,' the sang o the drooned bell. The waas were full o watter – still are, nae doot, like the hail toon. The sea cam roarin tae the shore, an it didnae stop. Scooped us up in yin muckle wallop. Woosh!

It wis a cheynge, though, doon there, a cheynge frae lyin in the hoose, in front o the telly aa day. A sittin duck, that wis me, ma legs frozen at birth. I couldnae move, couldnae speak – wurds aye got stuck hauf wey up the road tae ma thrapple. *Up* the road? Or doon? Whaur dae words come frae? Yer hert or yer brain? Weel, either wey, I could never get them past a feelin, or a thocht. I'd sit there on the sofa, watchin the blue licht frae the TV screen flicker ower ma Dad's face, like we were in an aquarium. I liked films aboot nature best, though they were aye tellin us there wisnae much o it left. The ice an perma-frost meltin, things dyin aa ower the place, like the sharks, wi their fins chopped aff fur soup. Aye – that's whit happens. I've seen it on the telly. Poor beasts. Just get chucked back intae the watter. Cannae swim nae mair wioot their fins. Dad liked the news, but he channel-hopped aa the time, pressin the remote. I couldnae tell him whit I wantit, whit I needit, just grunts cam oot ma mooth.

'Wheesht, will ye, for God's sake!' he'd snap at me. 'Gie's peace!'

He wis aye ratty, noo the fishin hud aa stopped. 'Nae fish left in the sea,' he'd say, 'aa fished oot.' He wis at a loose end, didnae ken whit tae dae wi hisel, or me. I'd finished at the school, an there wis a waitin list for the day centre, so I steyed at hame, week in, week oot.

We were sat there, me slumped on the sofa, thon last day when it aa happened, waitin fur ma mither tae come in frae wark. They propped me up wi cushions, but I'd aye slip doon. Ma bleedin hud stairtit – ma 'time o the month', Mum said. Ma hurdies were aa caked in bluid, an I wis girnin.

'Wheesht noo. Yer Mum winnae be lang. She'll sort ye.'

I gied anither wee whimper.

'I said will ye wheesht! See – I've missed it noo. Missed the news *again*.'

He picked up the remote, an flicked through the channels, openin a can o beer. 'Gie's peace, for God's sake – a wee break fur yince!'

A bloke wi professor specs is bletherin frae the screen, pyntin at a picture o shapes – stem cells, he said they were.

'Looks like somethin frae unner the sea,' says Dad. 'God, I'd gie the warld tae be oot there at the fishin again. I miss it, Christ, I dae, even the bitter cauld.'

The professor chunters on aboot 'identical daughter cells'. Dad gies me a look. I ken whit he's thinkin. I'm that wet an clarty doon ablow, I gie anither moan. He flips. Loses it aathegither:

'Aye, ye may weel moan! 'Identical daughter cells!' You're the fuckin identical daughter cell, the fuckin prison!'

I ken he aye thocht I wis a shackle, a chain, a cage for life. *I* wis the yin that should hae drooned, no ma wee twin sister. If only he'd taen *me* oot in the boat, no her. She went doon when he wisnae watchin, slippit ower the side, an they'd never fund her body. Ma mither couldnae forgie him. It wis like there wis a big hole in the faimily. She wis perfect, ma sister, but they'd landed up wi me, aa twistit an ma brain broke. He wis sabbin his guts oot, couldnae stop:

'A gap – I cannae fill it. Cannae fill the gap…'

I stairt tae whimper again, and he caums doon a bit.

'Och, I'm sorry, lassie, sorry. I dinnae ken whit's come ower me the day. It's just, I wis thinkin o yer sister – she'd be a wee wumman noo an aa…an she was that perfect. That bluidy perfect. Everythin where it should be… oh, God…'

Ma bleedin wis a milestane – I'm shair it mindit him o whit ma sister would hae been. An he wis scared. Scared o the bluid, haein tae clean me up, cause there wis nae wey I could sort masel oot. Twenty-fower seven job, me.

'Yer Mum'll be hame soon,' he says, blawin his nose, an wipin his tears. 'Come on, ma wee bauchle. We'll sing yer sang, will we? Fill in the gaps, eh? Like we used tae.'

An he cooried in next tae me. He still thocht o me as a bairn, an I liked it, in a kind o wey. The sang wi the gaps. I mind the day I first heard it. I wis just a wee bairn on his knee:

> There wis a man an he was mad,
> An he jumped intae a… (puddin bag).
> The puddin bag it wis sae fine,
> He jumped intae a bottle o… (wine).
> The bottle o wine it wis sae clear
> That he jumped intae a bottle o… (beer.)

I grunted in the gaps, and Mum wis aa excitit. 'She's tryin tae fill in the spaces! Listen! She kens the game! She's no a daftie – see, she's cottoned on!' They were that feart I wis brainless.

*An the bag o cotton caught on fire,*
*An blew him up tae Jeremiah – poof!*

That wis the sang ma Granda learned him, Dad said. An then he'd tell me the story o Jeremiah the prophet. How Jerusalem went up in smoke: Jeremiah – poof! Weel, it wisnae fire that did it tae *us*. Naw, it wis watter this time. I wunner if Jerusalem's still there? The Mount o Olives. I've seen it on the telly – mibbe too high tae go unner. But no oor wee toon. Richt on the shore, it wis. Mum aye said she hatit livin there. She wis frae the hills. 'The sea's eftir us,' she'd say, 'it's huntin us doon.' Hooses slidin intae the waves aa ower the coast. She aye wantit tae gang back tae the Hills o Hame – that's whit she cried the place she wis born, but too late – whoosh! We went unner.

An that wis me, clinkin aboot on the sea flair. A feast fur ma een, it wis, doon there, aa thay colours. I seen a dolphin giein birth, wi a midwife – anither dolphin, nudgin at the mither tae help the bairn on its wey. That's whit they dae. They're born tail first, dolphins, like me. Tail first, I wis, an fechtin – fechtin fur braith. Lack o oxygen, that's whit did fur me – couldnae get enough. Miracle I lived, they said.

Dinnae need it, though, when ye're a skeleton. Yon's the beauty o bein deid! Sometimes I'd watch the storms. The sea gets aa churned up. I got snagged on seaweed in ma first storm, an the seaweed got snagged on a shark's fin. We traivelled fur miles, landit in a graveyaird, a deid place whaur naethin lives. The sea flair wis littered wi oysters and crabs, just lyin there, nae life in them. The shark wis judderin, twistin an turnin. The beast couldnae breathe. Wi yin massive surge, it hauled itself oot thon hellish place, an we were back amang shoals o livin fish, their fins an tails slippin in an oot ma ribs like slivers o moonlicht.

I like sharks. They never bother ye. Fleet an sleek an strang. Till the knives get them, a nichtmare ye winnae believe till ye see the horror o it. Oh, I've seen it on the telly, lang syne, but it's no the same. The real thing's different aathegither. The ocean stairts tae dreep wi a daurk rain o cramasie bluid. Broken sharks wi nae fins come streamin doon frae the licht ontae the sea flair in a lifeless heap. I telt masel sic a nichtmare couldnae be real, that I'd wake up, an find masel back hame on the sofa.

I wunner whit happened tae Mum and Dad? Mibbe they were saved. They couldnae swim – typical fisherman, my Dad, an ma Mum wisnae much better. But they did their best fur me, used tae tak me tae the swimmin pool. I'd plowter aboot in the shallow end, them haudin me in the watter, tae get ma muscles relaxed. That's whaur I met him first, the lad I liked. At the pool. He couldnae speak neither. No wi his voice, onyroads. But he spoke wi his hauns. I'd been watchin him dive in, swimmin up an doon. He wis deif, niver turnt his heid when I grunted 'Hello'. That's how I kenned he couldnae hear. I had tae wait till he turnt roon, and then I smiled at him. He said 'Hello' wi his hauns. An I gruntit back. He had a foreign look, Eastern, wi almond eyes, high cheek banes, an bonnie.

'She's an awfy flirt,' says ma mither, aye apologisin fur me. She disnae even notice the laddie's deif. Guid job an aa, cause next thing ma Dad says tae me – an he disnae bother tae keep his voice doon: 'He's yin o they Arabs. You're no tae talk tae him. He's no oor type.'

The crap they come oot wi! Thank God the laddie couldnae hear. He just smiled, looked close intae ma eeen, real close, like he wis seein who I really am inside, an he said 'Hello' again, an then 'Goodbye' – sign language, same wey the speech therapists used tae, afore they gave up on me.

I saw him every week efter that, at the pool. He aye swam

ower tae me, an spoke wi his hauns an shinin een. I thocht aboot him aa the time, lyin at hame on the sofa, specially when I watched the wumman in the corner o the telly screen, signin the news. I wis shair he liked me. He kenned fine I wisnae a bairn. Ma breists had grown, nice an full an roon, an they looked guid in ma swimmin costume, if ye just looked at *them*, an no at ma twistit back an withered legs. I mind yince the laddie cam up real close, an pyntit tae his tap teeth, an then tae mine – we baith had a gap in the same place, right at the front!

'Whit a flirt,' ma mither said tae him. 'Dinnae encourage her.'

I wis supposed tae go swimmin on the day it happened, but ma mither said I'd tae miss it, wi this bein ma time o the month. She'd just come in wi a bag full o shoppin she'd picked up on the wey hame frae wark. There wis a low rummlin soond frae the street. The lichts went aff, an Dad got up tae hae a look oot the windae.

'Watter!' he scraiked. 'Waves o it, fuckin big waves o it!'

The watter crashed intae the hoose, like a muckle grey waa. I mind ma mither, her een an mooth like three black holes stampit intae her white face, ma faither raxin oot tae her. An that wis it. The sofa swept awa unner me, I wis tummlin, twistin, chokin, an then it aa went daurk.

I woke up ablow the sea, no a shred o flesh on ma banes – a white, clean-scrubbed skeleton. I wunnert whaur ma flesh had gaen. Had I been there sae lang it just fell awa, piece by piece, slaw, ower time, the saut watter, shells an saund scrapin ma banes clean? Or did some sea beasts swarm an strip them in a blink? Maybe I'd meet ma wee twin sister, but if I did, would I ken her – would she ken me? I mindit, frae photies at hame, she had a gap in her tap teeth an aa. We looked just the same frae the neck up. She'd be banes by then, like I wis, but smaa – she wis only a bairn when she drooned. But I niver fund anither skeleton on the ocean flair aa the time I wis doon there. I thocht I saw the shapes o humans float by abuin me, like shaddas in a dwaum. Yince, I saw a double bed, just the frame, its fancy brass fretwork laced wi seaweed; an a lanely plastic chair, like the yins they had at the doctor's surgery – electric blue, it wis, cowped on its back. I hoped ma sofa micht drift by. I missed it, ma sofa. Funny, that, the things ye miss.

Efter the first storm, I niver heard the kirk bell again. I must hae traivelled faur frae hame – the watter got caulder, an its colour cheynged – icy blue, sae pale it wis near tae white. Even ma deid banes could feel the chill. The creatures were different, strange fish I hudnae seen afore. Jagged forms o ice bergs sailed faur abuin whaur daylicht loomed. This maun be the end fur me, I thocht, ma mind dim wi cauld, the lang sleep at lest.

A dunt! A smack at ma jaw frae a thick piece o gless, ma heid reflectit in it. First time I'd seen ma face wioot skin. I looked a sair fricht, seaweed growin oot ma skull, like a wild bogle o the deep! I wis starin intae a lense, a camera that restit on a rock ledge. A cable snaked oot its tap, slidderin up intae the licht. The camera stairtit tae move. Ma lang seaweed hair wis aa fanklet in the cable, an pulled me up wi it. I streamed through faulds o mirk intae layers o licht, till ma skull hit the watter's surface.

There wis a scream, a shriek o terror. Frae the mooth o a man. He wis sittin in a boat, haudin the ither end o the cable. He tried tae pull ma seaweed hair awa frae it, but fricht at the sicht o a skeleton made him aa fingers an thumbs: the mair he panicked, the mair I got fanklet in the cable. Ma hauns were clink-clankin agin the side o the boat. He lifted his fit, an smashed his heel doon on ma fingers. The boat tipped, an ma left pinkie lowped intae the sea, like a wee white fish! The man seemed tae hae the notion I wis tryin tae sclim aboard. He drapped the camera ontae the deck, wi maist o the cable, but I wis still tied up in it, hingin ower the side. He switched on the engine, an we roared ower the sea, in and oot o ice floes. He kept lookin ower his shouther, een blin wi terror at the sicht o a skeleton flailin in his wake, seaweed streamin frae ma skull, like some crazed wumman that hud lost control o her watter skis!

We soon reached the shore, a grey stane beach, streakit wi thick, black ile, an littered wi carcasses o whales. He cut the engine, jumped intae the shallows, an dragged the boat ontae the stanes, leavin it there wi the deid beasts. Then he grabbed his camera, an ran ower a patchwork field o gress an ice, me hingin on tae the cable, clatterin ahint.

A mound appeared on the horizon, queer-like, antrin. Fur a mad moment, I thocht it wis a big, daurk bunnet! The nearer we cam, I could see it wis a hoose o sorts, built o skins. He took the camera inside, the cable attached, its lenth runnin unner the doorflap, me still fanklet in it, just dumped ootside.

'Whit God-forsaken place is this?' I thocht. 'Feels like we're the only fowk in the warld, him an me. But this is nae Gairden o Eden.' I lay there in a crumpled rauchle, ma banes aa mixter-maxter. There wis naethin aboot fur miles. An engine thrummed close by, dirlin through the grund intae ma skull. Soondit like a generator – ma Dad hud yin in the shed that made yon soond. I heard the man's braith heave ahint the skin waa. A blue licht flichtert through a gap in the doorflap. I lay fur ages on the ice. The colours o the sky were weird, like a yellow sickness lurked in it. A peelie-wallie sun slippit doon an restit on the horizon. The land o the midnicht sun, I mindit. But *which* land? There's a few whaur the sun disnae set in simmer. There wis a stirrin frae the hoose, an the man peeked oot the doorwey, checkin tae see if I wis still there. I heard the howl o a dug, or wolf, faur aff in the hauf nicht, hauf day. 'I hope yon beast winnae come fur ma banes,' I thocht.

But the man didnae seem tae hear. He wis still lookin at me, an I had a feelin I'd seen him afore, thay daurk een, but I couldnae mind whaur. Aathing in ma mindin wis dim, faur aff like the wolf's howl.

He steppit aa the wey ootside. Ma jaw wis thrust up oot the clarty seaweed that dreeped wi ile. I didnae ken whither tae lauch or greet, the mess I wis in. The look on the man's face cheynged. The fear meltit. He bent doon, pit oot his haun an touched the gap in ma tap teeth. A tear fell intae ma mooth frae his een. He liftit ma ain haun, an placed ma index finger-bane atween the gap in *his* tap teeth. Tears were rollin doon his cheeks, an I hud a sudden drouth oan me like a desert. I drank his tears, I drank them lang and lang, like aa the rivers on the planet are floodin through me. He gaithert up ma banes in his airms an cairried me intae the hoose.

We were unner a criss-cross dome o whales' jawbanes that were haudin up the skin waas. A fire burned frae a rusty ile drum in the middle o the hoose, an smoke rose through a flap at the tap o the dome. The man laid me on an auld double mattress, an slippit a bit rag ablow ma heid. His face looked like a ghaist in the licht o a computer screen. A silent film wis runnin on it – deid places on the ocean flair, like the graveyairds I'd seen doon there; sharks wi their fins sliced aff, bleedin slaw; birds streekit oot on a black shoreline, their wings aa clegged an clartit wi ile; muckle bens o ice – braw white cliffs, brakkin aff, an crashin intae the sea. He'd been filmin the daith o the warld, but wi nae soond – like aathing's deein wi nae voice, an there's naebody left tae see it, this story he's tellin, naebody but me – a skeleton.

He shut doon the screen, and looked at me wi thae daurk,

daurk een. He taen a knife oot his coat pocket, sliced the seaweed frae ma skull, an slaw, sae slaw, unfanklet ma banes frae the cable's grup. He stertit wi ma ribcage, then ma spine an pelvis, ma airms, legs, feet an hauns. He stroked the space whaur ma pinkie should hae been, wi sic a mortified look o shame I hud tae keep masel frae grinnin! He cradled ma skull close tae his breist, an stroked ma cheekbanes like I wis a new bairn, or lost lover. He never spak, but made saft soonds, giein signs wi his hauns: 'Hello,' 'wumman,' an 'swim'. I mindit then whaur I kent him frae – the laddie in the pool, afore the flood!

Next thing, he raxed fur a torch. The beam o licht wis weak, but he held it tae ma tap jaw, an scraped wi his knife at somethin steekit atween ma teeth. He scraped an scraped, carefu, patient, till the thing cam awa in his fingers – whit in the name o God? – money! A wee siller coin! I must hae picked it up doon in the sea. Imagine yon! – aa the cash pourin oot the banks wi the flood, waves o gowd an siller, yowdendrifts o bank notes, sinkin doon intae the deep. Like a muckle wishin well o the warld.

At lest he had me aa laid oot, an his smile telt me he liked the wey I looked. Ma spine wis straucht, wi nae hint o its auld twist, ma shouther blades like twa wings in perfect symmetry. He lay doon on his back aside me, real close, an turnt ma skull sidieweys, tae face him. Then he picked up yin o ma hauns, placed it on his breist, an fell asleep. I could feel his hert-beat, a drum aneath ma fingers. His ear aamaist touched ma mooth.

A high note, eldritch, like a wild wind frae the frozen North cam whistlin through ma teeth. Mibbe the note's pitch pierced a waa that hid the warld o soond frae his hearin – I dinna ken – but he seemed tae catch it through sleep, like he wis listenin. It wis the whisper o a sang, the sang o new life in ma banes, an wurds cam wi it. Wurds I could niver utter till noo, wurds that had aye been steekit in some daurk place inside me. I sang tae the man, as I lay there, sang fur flesh, warm flesh fur him tae touch, an me tae feel, breists an hips, lips an thighs, an a wame fur him tae fill. I sang fur sleek black hair tae sweep doon the hale lenth o ma lang white back.

In his sleep he heard me sing, an turnt ower. He stroked me, stroked ma new, saft skin, laced his fingers through ma hair, pit his lips tae mine, an drew the cover roon us baith.

'I dinnae ken the land I'm in,' I thocht, 'or whether this is birth or daith, but I've come hame.'

# Acknowledgements

The following stories have appeared in several publications: 'Bella Day' – *The Eildon Tree*; 'The Apple Tree' – *Gutter*; 'Chromosomes and Chocolate' – *Markings*; 'A Day Off' – *You Don't Look British* (Lumphanan Press); 'Skeleton Wumman' – *Southlight*. 'Letting Go' was broadcast on BBC Radio 4.

In 'Graves', the song quoted is 'Jock o Hazeldean' by Sir Walter Scott.

In 'Letting Go', the lines from Hamish Henderson's song 'Freedom Come All Ye' are reproduced with kind permission from Kätzel and Janet Henderson.

In 'Colour', the poem referred to is *'Die Kind Wat Dood Geskiet Is Deur Soldate By Nyanga'*/ 'The Child Who Was Shot Dead by Soldiers in Nyanga', by Ingrid Jonker; the lines from 'Donald Where's Your Troosers' by Andy Stewart are reproduced with the permission of the copyright holder, Kerr's Music Corporation Ltd; and 'Goin' Home' is by William Arms Fisher.

In 'The Apple Tree', the song *'Craobh nan Ubhal'* is an ancient Gaelic folk song, recorded by Flora MacNeil.

'Skeleton Wumman' is based on an Inuit folk tale – see the Story Museum:
https://www.storymuseum.org.uk/1001-stories/
skeleton-woman
There are several versions of the Skeleton Woman folk tale, the most well known told by CP Estés, in her book *Women*

*Who Run With Wolves*. My version is a contemporary retelling, partly inspired by the late, great young documentary filmmaker and conservationist, Rob Stewart, and includes the folk song 'There Was a Man and He Was Mad', recorded by Pete Seeger. The lines from Iain Crichton Smith's poem '*Tha thu air Aigeann m' Inntinn*'/'You Are At The Bottom of My Mind', are reproduced with the kind permission of Carcanet Press, Manchester, UK.

Thanks to Galina MacNeacail for permission to use her beautiful painting *Tree* as the cover image; to my beloved family for their generosity and support; to friends and neighbours, especially to Willie Lawson, who told me about the Prisoners of War he remembered at Robinsland Farm, West Linton; to Reverend Tom Burke who gave me information about Sir William Fergusson of Spittelhaugh, West Linton – assistant to the anatomist Dr Robert Knox and Sergeant-Surgeon to Queen Victoria; to Jim Aitken, Professor Meg Bateman, Dr Jamie Reid Baxter, Dr Michel Byrne, Liz Lochhead, James Robertson, Donald Smith and Alan Spence, for their editorial assistance and encouragement; to Paddy Byrne, Paola Dionisotti and Laura Maniero, my invaluable Italian consultants; and to the Pietrzyński family whom I miss, though I'm glad they took me to the best chocolate café in the world.

# Scots Glossary

Aa / aw – all
Aathegither – altogether
Aathing/ awthing – everything
Ablow – below
Abuin / abune – above
Aff – off
Afore – before
Agin – against
Ah / Ah'm – I / I'm
Aheid – ahead
Ahint – behind
Ain – (one's) own
Aince – once
Airm – arm
Alane / aa ma lane – alone, all alone
Amang – among
An – and
Ane – one
Anely – only
Askit – asked
Atween – between
Auld – old
Awa – away
Awfy – awful
Aye – always

Bairn – child
Baith – both
Bane – bone
Bauchle – hopeless thing
Bittie – little bit
Blackoot – blackout
Blawin – blowing
Bleester – a blistering storm
Bletherin – chatting
Blin – blind

Bluid – blood
Bocht – bought
Brae – slope, hillside
Brainch – branch
Braith – breath
Braw – fine, handsome
Breist – breast
Bricht – bright
Brocht – brought
Broo – brow
Brunt – burnt
Buckin – battering

Cairry – cairry
Cannae – can't
Cauld – cold
Caum – calm
Cheynge – change
Clarty – dirty
Clegged an clartit – clogged and dirtied
Clood – cloud
Cloot – a cloth
Coont/coonter – count/counter
Couldnae – couldn't
Cowped – knocked over
Cramasie – crimson

Dae/daein – do/doing
Daith – death
Daurk – dark
Deein – dying
Deid – dead
Deil – devil
Dinna/dinnae – don't
Dirl, dirlin – ring, ringing (as on stone)
Doon – down

Douce – gentle, sweet
Douk – dip, bathe
Drap – drop
Dreepin – dripping
Dreidfu – dreadful
Droon – drown
Dug – dog
Dunnelin – tolling
Dunt – hit, a blow
Dwaum – dream

Een – eyes
Efter – after
Eldritch – ghostly, weird
Erse – arse

Fae / frae – from
Faither – father
Falderals – fussy frills
Fankelt – entangled
Fantoush – flashy, stylish
Faulds – folds
Faur – far
Fecht / focht – fight / fought
Flair – floor
Flee – fly
Flichtert – flickered
Fortnicht – fortnight
Fouterin – fussing
Fower – four
Fowk – folk, people
Fund – found
Furst – first

Gaen – gone
Gaither – gather
Gaun – going
Gear – belongings
Gey – very
Gemm – game

Ghaist – ghost
Gie / gies – give / gives
Giein it laldy – being vigorous
Gless – glass
Gloamin – dusk
Goon – gown
Gowd / gowden – gold / golden
Greet – cry
Gress – grass
Grun – ground
Grup – grip
Guid – good

Haa – hall
Hae – have
Hale – whole
Hame – home
Hantle – a fair amount
Happit – wrapped
Hauns – hands
Haurd / haurdly – hard / hardly
Hee-haw – nothing
Heeze – hoist, heave
Heidit – headed
Herry – to plunder
Hert – heart
Hing – hang
Hirple – hobble
Hoose – house
Hoo – how
Howp – hope
Hud – had
Hus – has
Huvnae – haven't

Ile – oil
Insteid – instead
Ither – other
Iver – ever
Jaiket – jacket

# SCOTS GLOSSARY

Jalouse – guess
Juist – just
Jyned / jynts – joined / joints

Ken / kennin – know / knowing
Kirk – church

Lanely – lonely
Lang – long
Lang syne – long ago
Lauch – laugh
Lenth – length
Lest – last
Licht – light
Lik – like
Loot – let
Loup / lowp – leap

Ma – my
Mair – more
Maist / maislty – most /mostly
Maiter – matter
Mairry – marry
Mak – make
Masel – myself
Maun – must
Mibbe – maybe
Micht – might
Mindin – memory
Mirk – darkness
Moose – mouse
Muckle – much (ower muckle –
too much)
Mune – moon

Nae / Naw – no
Nane – none
Naewhaur – nowhere
Nicht – night
Niver – never

Noo – now

Oan – on
Ony / onyroad(s) – any / anyway
Ootby – outside
Oor – our / hour
Oorsel – ourselves
Ower – over

Peelie-wallie – pallid, sickly
Peyin / peyed – paying / paid
Photie – photo
Pit / pitttin – put / putting
Plowter – splash about
Poke – bag
Polis – police
Pooch – pocket
Pooer – power
Pynt – point

Quate – quiet

Rauchle – a muddle
Raxed – reached
Richt – right
Roon – round
Rummlin – rumbling

Sab – sob
Sae – so
Saft – soft
Sair – sore
Sang – song
Saut – salt
Sclim – climb
Scraikin – screeching
Semmit – vest
Shaddas in a dwaum – shadows in
a dream
Shair / shairly – sure/surely

Shoon/shuin – shoes
Shouthers – shoulders
Sidieweys – sideways
Siller – silver
Sin syne – since then
Slaw – slow
Slidderin – slithering
Sloomed – glided slowly
Smaa – small
Snaw – snow
Snawdraps – snowdrops
Socht – sought
Sookit – sucked
Soor – sour
Spreid – spread
Stairvin – starving
Stairtit – started
Stane – stone
Staun – stand
Steyed – stayed
Strang – strong
Streekit – stretched
Suld – should
Syne – then
Syped – seeped

Tae – to
Tak / takkin – take / taking
Tak tent – pay attention / take care
Tally – Italian
Telt – told
Ticht – tight
Thae – those
The day – today
Thegither – together
Thocht – thought
Thrapple – throat
T'ither – the other
Tousie – dishevelled

Traivelled – travelled
Tummlin – tumbling
Twa – two

Unfankelt – disentangled
Unner – under
Unnerstaun – understand

Vyce – voice

Waas – walls
Walcome – welcome
Wame – womb
Wark/warked – work/worked
Warld – world
Watter – water
Weel – well
Wey – way
Whan – when
Whaes – whose
Whaup – curlew
Whaur – where
Whit's – what is
Wi – with
Windae – window
Wis / wisnae – was / wasn't
Wrang – wrong
Wumman – woman
Wund – wind
Wurd – word

Yin / yince – one / once
Yon – that
Yont – beyond
Yowdendrifts – snow drifts

# Luath Press Limited

*committed to publishing well written books worth reading*

LUATH PRESS takes its name from Robert Burns, whose little collie Luath (*Gael*., swift or nimble) tripped up Jean Armour at a wedding and gave him the chance to speak to the woman who was to be his wife and the abiding love of his life. Burns called one of the 'Twa Dogs' Luath after Cuchullin's hunting dog in Ossian's *Fingal*. Luath Press was established in 1981 in the heart of Burns country, and is now based a few steps up the road from Burns' first lodgings on Edinburgh's Royal Mile. Luath offers you distinctive writing with a hint of unexpected pleasures.

Most bookshops in the UK, the US, Canada, Australia, New Zealand and parts of Europe, either carry our books in stock or can order them for you. To order direct from us, please send a £sterling cheque, postal order, international money order or your credit card details (number, address of cardholder and expiry date) to us at the address below. Please add post and packing as follows: UK – £1.00 per delivery address; overseas surface mail – £2.50 per delivery address; overseas airmail – £3.50 for the first book to each delivery address, plus £1.00 for each additional book by airmail to the same address. If your order is a gift, we will happily enclose your card or message at no extra charge.

**Luath** Press Limited
543/2 Castlehill
The Royal Mile
Edinburgh EH1 2ND
Scotland
Telephone: +44 (0)131 225 4326 (24 hours)
Email: sales@luath.co.uk
Website: www.luath.co.uk